you PROMISE

a novel

TAYLOR J. BRIDGEFORTH

JDMB Press

Also by Taylor J. Bridgeforth

Better Luck Next Time 1
Coming Up Dana 1.5

You Didn't Tell (a novella)

You Promise Book 1

you PROMISE

a novel

TAYLOR J. BRIDGEFORTH

YOU PROMISE
playlist

Special by SZA

"**Someone Else**" by ClockClock

"**Slow Burn**" by Janani K. Jha

"**Enemy**" (with JID) by Imagine Dragons

"**Try Again**" by Aaliyah

"**Let Me Down Slowly**" (feat. Alessia Cara) by Alec Benjamin

"**Lose Control**" by Teddy Swims

"**Baby, I'm Jealous** "(feat. Doja Cat) by Bebe Rexha

"**Beautiful Things**" by Benson Boone

"**Hero**" by Mariah Carey

"**squabble up**" by Kendrick Lamar

To me,

I'm proud of you

CHAPTER 1
Ava

"I don't HAVE to tell you anything," I say, scooting from Mitchell to the edge of my bed. I sleep in a twin, so there's not much room to get away. And even though my bedroom is lit only by the soft glow of Christmas lights, there sure isn't anywhere to hide.

"Well you better. Or else."

"Or else what?" I cross my arms and roll my neck.

The corner of his mouth ticks. "You know."

My body tenses. "I know you won't."

He leans in bringing us nose to nose. "Are you going to tell me or not?"

"Or. Not–AHHH!"

You'd think after four months of dating I'd take Mitchell's tickle threats seriously. However, I enjoy his hands on me in any way, shape, or form too much and am willing to risk the frantic kicks and little pee leaking out from laughter.

"Are you going to tell me or not, Ava," he teases.

I fight his lengthy fingers as long as I can until my face is pressed into my pillow and I can't take it anymore— "Okay. OKAY! I'll tell you."

"You'll tell me," he says, his five o'clock shadow grazing my cheek when I turn for breath.

I'm struggling under his chest trying to wriggle myself free from his sneaky fingers again. "AHHH—I said I'll tell you."

He stops. "You promise?"

My skin tingles at his breath near my ear. "I promise."

Mitchell pulls me up to sit on his lap, locking his chocolate eyes to mine. "I'm waiting."

I straighten my posture, clear my throat, and steady myself by anchoring my arms around his neck, smoothing my hand down the nape of his fade. "If you must know—"

"I must," he says, fanning my braids off one shoulder.

I glare at him and with a heavy breath admit, "I do not like chocolate."

"Like you're allergic," he asks caressing my lower back.

"Like I think it tastes like shit."

He stops. "Wow. Really?" I nod. "So what have you done with four months worth of chocolate?"

I feign innocence. "Casey has a sweet tooth."

Mitchell's eyebrows come together. "I've been buying chocolates for a dude?"

I snort. "If it counts for anything, I think it got you on Casey's good side."

Casey is my life long best friend. Placed in the same foster home—the only home we ever knew, we attached ourselves to each other quick and it has been the same ever since. He knows me better than anyone. Friend or beau can't get too close to me before going through Casey first.

"I don't care about being on Casey's good side. I care about being on *your* good side."

He grips my hips and I lean my lips into his, parting his mouth with my tongue. Mitchell wraps his arms around my waist and lays me on my back across the bed. His lips move from mine and down toward my breastbone over my T-shirt. He nips around my chest and I let out a moan as he makes his way back up. "Mission accomplished," I say.

Mitchell laughs into the crook of my neck then breathes me in.

When he doesn't move I ask, "You good?"

He keeps his head lowered. "Mhmm," he murmurs into my skin.

I don't like the way he's hiding from me. My hands prickle and I smooth them down the length of Mitchell's T-shirt, masking my discomfort as solace for him. "You can tell me."

I count to almost 40 in my head before he turns to the side of my face to say, "I love you, Ava."

Whoa. My arms go slack and I freeze beneath him. My true feelings for Mitchell have been perched on the tip of my tongue waiting for him to tell me first. I had to believe he was saying he loved me by his own volition not by force if he wasn't ready.

"Did you hear me," he asks.

"Uh...er—Did *you* hear you?"

Mitchell hovers above me on his elbows. I hold his face in my hands and sweep my thumbs along his amber cheeks, while he combs his fingers through the ends of my box braids.

"Say it again," I say. He opens his mouth and I silence him with my finger at his lips. "Only if you mean it."

He nods. "I love you, Ava. I mean it."

I wrap my legs around his waist and my arms around his neck, securing him to me, absorbing his words. "You promise?"

"Mhmm, I love you." His lips linger against my cheek. "Are you going to say it back?"

"Sure will." I don't. Mitchell raises his head to look at me—a soft flush tanning his brown cheeks. "If you're here in the morning."

"Why wouldn't I be?"

I shrug. I could lean into the possibility of my luck finally turning around. Except I'm not easily swayed by sweet words—not anymore.

"How about we focus on what we're gonna do tonight," I say.

"Which is?"

I peep between us, pressed together like Pringles in a can, before looking into Mitchell's darkening brown eyes. "Moving from second base and straight to home."

Mitchell lifts our tangled bodies from the bed and slams us to the center, both of us fighting to remove the others clothes, a quick slip of the condom before we meet with an exhale and hearty groan.

"Hi...Ava..."

I looked around my locker to Eli Jacobson—Central North High School varsity soccer captain, his green eyes glued to his shoes.

"Eli?"

"Yea, hi."

Eli Jacobson, star athlete, not super tall, all muscle, with veins popping out along his year-round tanned arms and legs.

"Hi." I said it like a question, and straightened my posture to exude confidence in front of one of the most popular guys in school.

"Ava, I was wondering if you'd like to meet me for lunch tomorrow?"

I fell back against the cool red steel of my locker to simmer the flames my body ignited. Eli Jacobson asked me out for lunch? Even though I've known him since seventh grade, the most we've ever said to each other was freshman year when paired to dissect a frog.

Eli: This is gross.

Me: Don't worry. I'll do it.

We got an A.

"Oh." I blushed, not caring about the change in our limited repertoire. "Yea, of course."

Eli attempted to meet my now wavering eye. "So you'll meet me at our table—the soccer table, I mean..."

"Yea, I know where," I said with a smile.

"I'll see you then."

"Yup. Okay."

Eli took his hands out of his pockets and walked away with a small wave. I struggled to keep my feet planted until he turned the corner. When he walked far enough, i.e. five steps, I slammed my locker closed and rushed to the library where I knew I'd find Casey.

"No running Miss Hill."

I stopped short at the school librarian's tone, gifted her a wee smile, then resumed power walking toward my best friend.

Right where I knew he would be with his nose in a book, I pulled out the chair opposite Casey and flopped in.

"Ava," Casey said with a page turn.

"Guess what?"

"Hmm."

"Eli Jacobson asked me to eat lunch with him tomorrow."

He still hadn't looked up. What's with boys not knowing how to hold eye contact. "Oh really?"

I knocked on his book to gain his attention. He reluctantly brought his eyes to mine. "Yes, really! I am going to sit beside—or should I sit across? Hmm." I deliberated the optics as my finger tapped my chin... "Moral of the story, I'll be sitting with Eli Jacobson tomorrow at lunch."

"Why do you have to say his first and last name?"

"Hello! Eli Jacobs—" Casey rolled his eyes. "Eli plays varsity soccer."

"And you like soccer now?"

"I like soccer players who invite me to lunch." Casey went back to his book. I snatched it away, closed it, and held it to my chest. "Be excited for me."

He looked up, ran a hand over his Jean-Michel Basquiat inspired locs, and leaned back with his arms crossed. "Why?"

"Ugh, don't you get it. First it's lunch with Eli Jacobson and then there's Homecoming with Eli Jacobson. We'll go to Indiana University upon graduation, I'll major in some sort of liberal arts, he'll join men's soccer. I'll graduate summa cum lade and

Eli Jacobson will sign a contract with FC Cincinnati and all will be right in the world."

"And where do I fit into this fairy tale?"

"Duh...um. First, ask Mo Tang to Homecoming."

Casey crunched his nose. "Pass."

"Well, you don't need to worry about anything now. Now, I have to get through lunch tomorrow."

The overhead bell rang. Casey stood and retrieved his book from my arms. "No, now we have to go to Health."

I stood as well, standing a mere six inches below Casey's six foot frame. "Will you help me find something to wear?"

"We don't have much," he said, palming his free locs in front of his eyes, landing down his sepia toned face.

I deflated and looped my arm through his on our way out the library. "Don't remind me. I'm hoping if I spend a good 45 minutes on the stain from my skirt your good friend Rayvin returned—"

"She's your friend too," he said. I clenched my teeth against his unwavering defense of his girlfriend who takes what she wants without asking and without returning it the same way she found it.

"If I can get the skirt clean, come tomorrow afternoon I'll be a madam of poise and style," I said, pretending to wave like Julie Andrews from The Princess Diaries.

"Good plan."

I leaned into Casey's shoulder dreamingly. "19 hours and counting."

19 HOURS LATER.

I stood outside the cafeteria as other students rushed past me. Once the bell rang, I entered so everyone knew I, Ava Hill, was headed to eat lunch with Eli Jacobson at the soccer table. Having spent an hour and a half last night, I was able to treat the stain on my denim skirt and paired it with a blue V-neck top I had to tuck in due to the hole along the seam. The preparation anxiety left me because the time was now. I was fit and ready.

I counted to twenty and pulled the door open to the masses seated at various wooden tables with our always questionable cafeteria food. I kept my shoulders back and chin high as I made my way to the soccer table. The eyes of my peers were stuck on me as I made my way down the aisle. My smile faltered when I got to the table the soccer team usually sat was empty.

I kept walking to pretend I knew what I was doing and saw the team at a table they've never sat at before. I made my way over and searched for Eli.

"Hey guys, why are you over here?"

"We always are," said Tanner. He smirked into his sandwich with his other teammates.

"Oh, right," I said. After I cleared my throat, I asked, "Well, where's Eli?"

"Why're you asking?"

The more they laughed, the harder my teeth sunk into my bottom lip. "We're supposed—we're having lunch together today."

Tanner nodded his chin over my shoulder. "Actually, he's having lunch with Amber Delgado."

I whipped around to Eli seated across from Amber Delgado, their conversation having captured his full attention. "Oh." I turned my back from Eli and Amber, to the soccer team on the verge of hysterics from my growing wince. I walked away from their table then ran out of the cafeteria and their exploded fits of laughter as my eyes watered.

By the time I found Casey in the library my cheeks were soaked and my boldness had crumbled.

"How was lunch with Eli Jacobson," he said into his book.

"He's eating lunch with Amber Delgado."

Casey noticed my tone and then my puffy face when he looked up. "What?"

I pulled out the chair and sat next to him. "It was a joke—all a joke. I'm a joke."

Casey stood and wrapped his arms around me as I sobbed into his chest. "That's not true. Eli is a manipulator and you don't deserve someone who'd treat you this way. I'm so sorry Ava."

"I feel like such a fool. Homecoming, IU, Cincy—what was I thinking? I'm such an idiot."

"Nothing is wrong with dreaming, Ava. You just can't count all your chickens before they hatch."

I sniffed. "Fuck chickens and fuck Eli Jacobson."

"Fuck chickens and fuck Eli Jacobson," Casey repeated and kissed the top of my head. I pulled him tighter knowing he'd always be there for me as a friend. And it would have to be enough.

I awaken in my bed the next morning to the smell of something sweet—vanilla or brown sugar—which is ten times better than what I'm waking up from. I rub my eyes from one of the worst haunting memories of my dreaded high school experience and roll over to the cold space Mitchell must have vacated—I sniff again and my mouth waters. Mitchell got up and made breakfast? Okay, I officially believe him—Mitchell Scott loves me. I hide my smile behind my hands, then turn over to squeal into my pillow before getting up out of bed and joining Mitchell in the kitchen.

When I round the corner from the hallway, Casey and I collide, him barely holding on to his plate of food.

"Plate to go?" I snatch a piece of bacon from his breakfast and pop it in my mouth—wiping the extra grease on my fingertips down my pajama shorts. "Mmm. Good idea. Where's Mitchell?"

Casey hooks a thumb over his shoulder. Great. I pull him into the hallway and shove him against the wall, unable to keep from bouncing, "Mitchell told me he loved me last night and he's here this morning." I jump with two soft claps. "He's here and made breakfast for me and I'm so happy you got a plate. Now, go to your room, close the door, and I'll knock twice when it's safe to come out. Yes—"

"Ava."

"Good. Shoo." I push him down the hall, yank my bonnet off my head, to throw into my room. I comb my fingers through my braids to land across each shoulder, and I turn the corner to enter...an empty kitchen.

Hmm, no big deal, Mitchell is most likely in the bathroom. I walk along the counter, picking blueberries from the container and popping them into my mouth, vibrating with giddiness.

"Ava," Casey says, back in the kitchen, still holding on to his plate.

I keep my eyes from rolling and ask, "What?" I directed Casey to his bedroom so he wouldn't see me mounting Mitchell in love and gratitude and if he doesn't leave soon, he will.

"Mitchell isn't here."

"Obviously. He's in the bathroom and you must be going to your room so I can thank him appropriately." I thrust my hips into the corner of the counter.

"Ava, I was bringing this plate to you. I made breakfast. I thought you'd need it because..." He sets the plate down. "Mitchell left last night and he hasn't been back."

Casey's locs covering his face and his all black attire has him looking like the Grim Reaper; and the reality of what he's saying slowly devours me.

Mitchell left last night?

No.

No.

No.

And he hasn't been back.

No sane man would tell someone he loves them, to leave in the middle of the night.

No.

"No," I say.

Casey's eyes are soft. "It's true."

"No, not this time. Not again. No, because this time I did it right. I wasn't clingy, I was funny, and I let him discover his feelings before detailing mine. Mitchell was supposed to stay, he was..." My breaths choke. "He was...he was suppo...sed—supposed to...stay. Not...again..." Not enough oxygen is getting to my brain to keep me upright, I reach out for balance, miss the counter and fall.

Casey calling my name is the last thing I hear before my world goes dark.

Chapter 2
Ava

A semi-damp cloth is on my forehead when I slowly blink my eyes open. It doesn't take long for the truth to wash over me again: Mitchell's baseless confession knowing he wouldn't be in my bed the following day for me to say it back. Tears seep out the corners of my eyes at my stupidity.

"Are you awake?"

I roll over to my side to Casey laying on my bedroom floor looking up at me. I don't know what time it is or how much time has passed since the morning blackout. I do know it's too soon for Casey's placating. *The way they treat you is an expression of how they see themselves, not you. Another frog closer to your prince.* Blahblahblah. I've lived the same story with a different man for too long and it's time to realize I am the problem.

Casey comes up on his knees and shuffles to the side of my bed. His palm cups my cheek and his thumb wipes the residue from my tears. "I need your help," he says.

I pause. Just because I *thought* I wasn't in the mood to be appeased doesn't mean I expected not even a smidge of sympathy. Okay, yes, Casey seemingly caught me on the way down to the floor, brought me to my bedroom, and put a wet cloth on my head; now we're supposed to have copious amounts of cookie dough and blending into the couch while watching the *Mission Impossible* series.

"Ava, I don't have time to bring you back to life with calorie ridden cookie dough and Tom Cruise." *Okay, damn.* "I need your help."

I heard him and now I'm seeing him. Casey's eyes are serious and dark behind his hair, his mouth in a hard line. He's not an animated person by any means and his usual gray skies have transitioned to thunder clouds. I cannot imagine what has happened for Casey to need me. He's never needed anyone. My erratic emotions over what I could have done to have Mitchell sneak out in the middle of the night are on hold because the only time Casey's dim goes dark is when it comes to his biological family.

Myself and a large majority of us who grew up in foster care with Miss Green accepted whatever family we had were not coming back. Casey on the other hand, couldn't grasp his family dropped him off and never looked back. He's spent his entire life looking for answers and coming up with dead ends: wrong address, same last name—different lineage, death.

I got over the fact my birth mother prostituted her way through life before someone didn't take no for an answer. I was born and barely thought of again, and decided a long time ago to give her the same courtesy. My only drawback is the dream—my dream. I want a husband and kids with a St. Bernard. I have strong reasoning to bury my dreams like I buried the thought of my birth mother; unfortunately, I've been suckered into the thought of romance with books written by Nicola Yoon, Beverly Jenkins, and Tia Williams.

Believing in love is what hurts me over and over. Casey has only been hurt by love once and I will be there for him as he's always been there for me.

I come up, my legs hanging off the bed. "Casey, what's wrong?"

Casey stands and walks towards my bedroom door. "Follow me."

I wrap myself in my robe and trail behind him without a clue. When I pass the kitchen, I look away from what I thought was a grand gesture from Mitchell. Our small dining room table is lit by the ceiling lamp rather than the sun beaming through the window and I realize I've lost the entire day. I lower myself into the chair with caution among the littered papers and manila envelopes. Casey takes the opposite seat, and I wait for him to explain whatever I'm sure will change the trajectory of our lives.

"Ava, I need you to promise me...whatever I ask of you, you will do. No questions asked. I need you to be my person on this one. Please. Just this once and I'll never ask anything of you again."

I nod. "Okay."

"You promise?"

Casey takes a promise as serious as going to the dentist twice a year. No matter how big or small, agreeing to a promise is a verbal contract. Breaking a promise to Casey is like breaking my heart, we lose ourselves. Casey has lost enough people and patience hoping for change to last a lifetime. I'm the sole person he's always believed in.

"Yes Casey, I promise."

His tense shoulders drop a fraction. "I found something."

Oh shit. This can only mean one thing. After years as an underpaid and overworked security guard in various buildings and stores, Casey got a job in cyber security at a large building with shady men in expensive suits. These men didn't care if he went to college. Casey taught himself the inner workings of cyber security and then some. With the proper equipment, he had all of the resources to unearth his past.

He releases a deep breath and opens a manila envelope and places it in front of me. My palms sweat as I shuffle through the various documents and pictures clipped together. I take my time scanning through the information Casey gave me because what I'm seeing can't be true. Can't be what Casey has been holding out his entire life for.

For the first time, I feel Casey's heartbreak instead of my own. The documents conclude Casey's lifelong mission: answers regarding his birth family.

He always assumed his family abandoned him the way most of us were abandoned—dropped off and never looked back, convincing ourselves it's easier than being unloved, while silently questioning why. The material in front of me is Casey's worst nightmare. Casey Roberts, my best friend; the most handsome, kind and smartest guy in my world who deserves not a damn thing he's ever gone through to survive was in fact, unloved.

February 23, 2001, Shawn and Toni Roberts welcomed Cole Tace Roberts—born 11:53pm and Casey Shea Roberts—born 11:58pm into the world and only Cole Tace Roberts into their lives. He found family pictures of a child the exact replica as my best friend, a perfect mixture of his parents hugging and loving their son.

As I grip Casey's birth certificate, I concede right now whatever this promise for Casey entails, he has my full support.

"Ava, I know it's not much—"

"Casey, what do you mean? This is your birth certificate..." Wait. "Right? This is your birth certificate?" I wave the flimsy paper in front of his face.

Maybe—we have to take into account how this could be another dead end. Casey has put himself through hell since being able to navigate the Internet and the amount of information it provides. Parents do not have kids to split them up or only take one home. People are not crazy and selfish to this extent. What could have possibly been wrong with Casey and where is Cole? *Who* is Cole?

Casey snatches the worn piece of paper from my fingers and holds it against his chest, protecting himself and the only valuable information about his birth family away from me.

"You think I've taken all this time to *think* this is it? This is it," Casey yells and I flinch from his words spitting on my face.

Casey isn't prone to yell no matter how angry, this is pain. No one is immune to pain. Casey doesn't endure pain, he reacts.

One specific, though unforgettable occasion, Casey's reaction to unbearable pain almost led to his complete undoing. He vowed then to never let himself lose control again. Right now, pain is vibrating throughout his entire body when it usually follows him like a shadow.

"I'm so sorry Casey. We could have never thought..." Doesn't matter what we thought, this is life now. "You don't deserve this."

Casey gathers his documents back into the manila envelope without looking at me. I didn't doubt him or his research, I doubt mankind. There's always a new level of cruel someone finds to commit.

Casey jumps out of his chair, ready to take on the world by himself as usual. Not this time. This is too much for Casey to take on. I grab his wrist to stop him from getting to far away, physically and emotionally. Thankfully, he halts at my touch.

Talking to our worn linoleum, he says, "Ava, I have a plan—a plan to help me understand what all I have missed out on about my parents and my...twin brother." Casey bursts out in laughter. "My twin brother." He's in shock. "That's all I want. I want to know where I went wrong."

I stand, and lift his chin to see me. "Casey, you didn't do anything wrong. You were conceived by two evil and weak minded people who missed out on the best son they would've ever had and—"

He swats my hand away. "I don't need to be placated right now, Ava! I have a plan and you promised you'd do it no questions asked," Casey says, his dark brown eyes boring into mine.

I simply nod. I am both determined and frightened about what I've agreed to. Casey's temperament is like a pot set to simmer, boiling beneath the surface. He's found the facts, not the reason, and I'm not sure how he'll respond when faced with the truth. However, I did make a promise and I plan to follow through. When I think of Shawn and Toni Roberts and what they did to their family, my allegiance is solidified.

CHAPTER 3
Ava

Three weeks later, Casey moved me out of the house we've shared for five years and into a luxury apartment on Mass Ave in the middle of an Indianapolis winter: a mix of black ice, slush, harsh winds and negative degrees.

I balked at what this could cost him considering the location and the amenities and he rebuffed me, calling it a thank you gift. I know my salary at the Humane Society keeps us at the house that's drafty in the winter, muggy in the summer, with a number of electrical wires loose due to the constant flickering lights—and I have a bit of pride to not accept handouts from my best friend.

However, a room to myself is one thing. 653sq ft is something I've only dreamed about, until now. For now. I can't live away from Casey forever.

Of course, I tried to convince Casey to send Cole a direct message on Instagram and invite him to coffee, except it's not that simple. The thought of confronting your long lost twin isn't easy.

So instead we settled on a couple of months of amateur sleuthing resulting in a new family reunited—what could go wrong?

Since almost everyone has a social media profile to brag humbly from, Casey and I have been gathering all we can on Cole Tace Roberts. He graduated from Butler University in 2023. Since writing on his school newspaper in high school and college, Cole graduated with an English and Creative Writing degree and went from an interim writer to full time writer writing short stories for Speck, a literary magazine and upcoming small press.

Cole checks in weekly to Bovaconti Coffee and local dive bar, The Falcon, and is regularly seen with a friend he calls Nugget. Casey wasn't able to find his real name. I'm still sick to my stomach about Casey having a twin brother and them living separate and different lives. Through pictures on Cole's Instagram, Casey and Cole look exactly alike: reddish brown skin, disconnected goatee, and a healthy set of teeth. With all their similarities, I can't find the difference between the two so how could their parents? What made them decide which child to raise as their own?

Casey grew up scorned and always scared of people leaving him. As I've always been a hopeless romantic, Casey would barely let his emotions get the better of him. He thinks it'd prove him to be weak. I've tried to soften his heart by explaining how a life without love is a life unlived and he simply reminded me of my exhausting list of failed relationships. I couldn't defend myself without proof.

Casey doesn't believe love is in the cards for people like us: orphans, damaged, invisible. While I still believe in a man taking it upon himself to build my dream house and write me letters everyday for a year. I've read and seen *The Notebook* too many times.

I read books and Casey reads people for who they are whether good or bad. After finding out the information about his family Casey isn't going to believe in 'good' people anytime soon.

Casey enters my new apartment tainting the smell of fresh paint with the aroma of cigarette smoke clinging to his signature all black clothing. His head is hung as I finish reading up on Cole for the day. He sinks into the couch and scowls at Cole's face on the screen. I close and place my aged laptop on the coffee table. Casey isn't okay. I fear he'll never be okay again. The information he wanted to uncover was supposed to bring him answers, instead its brought more questions. When I slowly reach for his hand, he pulls away from me—again. Casey and I have shifted from the comfort of best friendship to the tension of truth, I need my best friend. I plead whatever I'm able to find out about his parents will set him free.

"Casey, I think I'm ready," I say.

He shifts so one leg is propped on the cushion. "Are you sure?"

I nod and reach for his hand again. This time he lets me hold a part of him. "I want to help you get all the information you need to...to move on. I'm thankful for the apartment and your trust in me but I want my best friend back and the only way that'll happen is when you get the truth, right?" Casey looks away. "You deserve the truth."

He sniffs and wipes under his nose with his sleeve. "Okay...And thank you. Thank you for doing this for me. I don't think I've thanked you yet. And I'll never be able to thank you enough, Ava."

I slide closer to Casey and take his face in my hands, giving him my all through our locked eyes, letting him know this pursuit is as important to me as him. "Tomorrow, I'm going to meet Cole and attempt to make him fall in love with me so he'll tell me his secrets."

"You make it sound like this will be easy for you, Ava." Casey's cynicism burns and I remove my hand from him.

My throat burns. "Yea, well, I plan on mirroring my previous jackass relationships. Mitchell, for example." I force a laugh through my teeth. "He listened to everything before sneaking out. And this time Cole will be the blubbering idiot talking about his dreams and goals and how he—"

Casey clears his throat and I stop. Casey's thought process is if Cole falls for me, he'll divulge what Casey needs to know. What Casey doesn't know is I don't believe in myself for Cole to fall in love with me. No one ever has. They've all ghosted, lied or cheated. No one has ever stayed and I have to make sure Cole stays.

Picking invisible lint from the couch fresh out of the box, I confess, "Case, what if Cole doesn't trust me enough to fall in—or love me enough to trust—you know I don't...how I have zero luck when it comes to relationships and ours is the most important to me. This has to go to plan."

"Ava, what you need to believe right now is no matter how you've been treated over the years, you deserve all you've ever dreamed. The three bedroom house, husband with two kids and Henry." My heart warms like he knew it would from his words. Casey's thumb catches a happy tear before it's able to roll down my cheek. "You, Ava Hill are more than enough."

I lean into his hand and absorb his magic words making me feel deserving.

"Thank you, Casey."

Casey moves his arm across my shoulder, we fall back into the cushion with my head on his chest. "Ava, if you had the confidence I see you're capable of you'd never have to question yourself." He kisses my hair. "Any questions about the plan?"

Still sore from the past and focused on the future, I sniff, "I think I get it."

Casey jumps up from the couch, pulling me up with him by my arms.

"No, Ava! You have to know—*make* Cole fall in love with you," he spits. I fight out of his hardy grip.

"OW! Casey!"

He blinks out of his temper and releases me. Exactly what I was afraid of, Casey is too sensitive and attached to finding out answers. He's gone from a simmer to boil and I have to try to keep the lid from popping off.

I'm also not proud of the first thought that occurred to me when he grabbed me. Growing up in foster care, we're inherently gullible, which can lead to being taken advantage of; physically, mentally, emotionally, it doesn't matter. Which is why Miss Green made sure, us girls specifically, we knew how to defend ourselves. Whereas, most of the guys found comfort at the shooting range, Casey included. Another temporary perk of our new living situation, I don't have to think about my apartment being robbed and them running off with a loaded gun in my roommates name.

Thanks to Miss Green, I've only had to lay someone out a handful of times in my life, Casey has never came close...

His hands slam to his sides. "Fuck, I'm sorry. I'm so sorry, Ava. I didn't—I don't know..." He wipes his hands down his face. "I don't want any surprises. You have to trust me—I won't let Cole hurt you."

"I trust you, Casey." And I do. I have to be careful with his emotions. This is an especially tender situation and I can't blame Casey for how he reacts. We're both fish out of water.

He loosens. "Good."

I crack my fingers with my thumb. No matter how ready I am, there is a part of me that already feels for Cole Tace Roberts. I've been Cole, I've fallen for people who only pretended to reciprocate. It's going to ruin him. Intentionally damaging someone isn't something I'm used to.

"I know this is a lot, Ava. I don't want you to get confused with what I'm asking you to do and how you'll *act,*" he emphasizes at the end. I got it. I am playing a role, nothing else. "When was the last time you talked to Blaine?"

I stiffen. Blaine is more than a friend and less than a therapist. He'd visit Miss Green's and be with us kids who felt abandoned by the world. It would go from watching an aged movie to spilling our hopes and dreams, or lack there of. I took to Blaine quickly because he would help me spin tales to enhance my imagination; as well as, letting me know when my fantasies stretched too far.

"I missed his call about a week ago," I say.

"And your last slip?"

I take a step back with a dry mouth. "Casey, it's been…a long time."

Casey closes the gap I created. "You can't lie to me, Ava. I know you've been in contact with Paul."

Paul was another one of Miss Green's children until he didn't come home before curfew one too many times and got kicked out. He then lived unhoused until he was able to support himself by selling hallucinogens for one of Indianapolis' well known drug dealers.

My cheeks grow hot. "I didn't go through with it."

"Give me your phone," Casey says.

I don't look up, clocking my phone at the edge of the middle table. Casey goes for it, and knowing my passcode his thumbs skirt across the screen. Deleting Paul's number, I'd venture.

Casey hands my phone back to me. I take it and throw it on the couch.

"I know his number by heart," I say.

"And I know you won't call him. Right?"

I don't answer.

"Call Blaine instead. And go in to see him soon—without telling him what we're doing. He's prone to stopping us from having fun."

I nod around a smile. With few things to keep us busy at Miss Green's all we had was our curiosity and Casey's is expansive. Illegal fireworks resulting in the backyard shed catching on fire. Eyedrops in the older kids drinks who ate all of the day old dessert. And we usually fabricated an alibi before Blaine could catch us.

Casey steps and kisses me lightly on the forehead. He walks around with the weight of an elephant crushing his hopes and dreams; physically he's as light as a feather.

"I'm ready, Casey. I promise." Casey stares me down. "I won't fuck up," I add to convince him and myself.

Lord give me strength, tomorrow I come face to face with Cole Roberts. Imminent heartbreak, to be announced.

CHAPTER 4
Cole

I don't know what's more distracting, my anxious knee jumping up and down or Nugget aggressively playing his Switch. Another cup of caffeine and I'm sure my stress will settle. Third cups a charm. I stare at the counter waiting to hear my name to get my hands on another hot chocolate with extra whip cream. Shivering against the Valentine decor covering the glass window we're placed in front of, I fail not to think about my recent breakup with Rachel.

It's only been three months sans-Rachel. I knew we wouldn't be 'and I now announce you man and wife.' I was cool in her company and she was dependent on mine. However, when I did the math, Rachel and I were together for eight months. Twenty-two days post-breakup she was on Instagram showing off her new boyfriend as 'the best Christmas present E-V-E-R.' That was mortifying to relay to my friends.

"No, no, no—" Nugget mummers, slamming his padded covered Switch against the table—thus tearing me away from an impossible math equation.

As addictive as MarioKart is, Nugget has been trying his darnedest to get first place against player 'gonnagetcha' disguised as Miss Peach. This is how he spends his days; avid gamer by day and stand-up comedian by night. Funny enough, my best friend graduated with an engineering degree but found making sketches on TikTok and comedy sets at colleges to be more lucrative.

Unlike myself, where I continue to put my ass on the line trying to get published by Speck. Speck is a local indie press specializing in quarterly print zines, online short stories, and they've recently started building their clientele for manuscripts. As much as they fancy my short stories, my boss is looking for an entire novel and I can't write anything more than 8,000 words.

The hustle and bustle of a coffee shop usually serves as white noise I use to write fervently. Unfortunately, as soon as my boss asked for a manuscript—any and everything has taken my attention away from writing.

"Dammit, dammit—" Nugget throws his Switch on the table and I reach out and catch it before it falls off the edge.

I place it in my lap to give him a moment to calm down and myself the chance to put words into sentences. I've been on the same hanging sentence since we got here two hours ago.

"Give it back," he says.

"Not yet."

Nugget hmphs back in his chair with his arms crossed. "Now?"

"Hush."

"No. I want it back. Give it back." He regresses to reaching across the table and tapping my shoulder incessantly. "NowNowNowNowNow—"

I have to be stronger than him. I have to be stronger than him, I repeat in my head.

"NowNowRightNowNowNow—"

I take the game from my lap and throw it at his head.

"Ow, damn dude," he says.

"You deserved it."

"Not the assault and battery—you'll be hearing from my lawyer."

I snicker, sure I could convince his lawyer to see my side of things.

"I mean it. I'm as serious as...Fresh. Meat."

"What is serious as fresh meat," I ask.

"You'd know if you ever looked up from your computer. Me-ow," he purrs.

"Don't purr."

Nugget, my best friend of 15 years, is the guy women eventually go for, after wearing them down a bit. He's a 200lb redhead with comedic timing and no filter. What woman doesn't like to laugh and pure honesty?

I sigh. "It's really hard to concentrate when you purr at the women who walk in—"

"Dibs on her—only her. And in case she says no when I ask her out, dibs on the two I called before her. To soak my woes."

I laugh. Nugget's always been a character; a cartoon character. He stands to head toward his new target when Joe, our usual barista, finally calls my name. With Nugget's first step, he trips on the table leg, catching himself by falling back in his chair. Even if no one else noticed, I point and laugh at his pink cheeks as I get up.

I place a period somewhere it may or may not belong and make my way to the counter to retrieve my new drink. Coming up too close and fast to the woman in front of me, she turns right into my chest which connects with her iced—iced? It's the middle of February—coffee. The cold beverage swims down my T-shirt and into my jeans.

"Aww, fu..." I press my lips together to keep from cursing and take quick breaths.

"Oh shit, I'm so sorry," she says.

Cold. So so cold. The woman turns back and forth, patting me down with napkins from my chin to my chest. I catch her hand before she reaches my belt. She fights me then stills. When her eyes lock with mine, she's scowling before her eyebrows relax and my breath catches. What a beautiful and illuminating woman. Big brown eyes, complexion similar to mine with a hint of gold matching her nose ring. Her box braids frame her face with her edges laid all around. And her lips: pouty, full, moisturized.

She snatches her hands from mine and I take a step back.

"I am so sorry," she says. Her eyes are shining to fight back oncoming tears. She's upset with herself for no reason. Unless she were to reject my dinner invitation. I think I'll take her first to Italian and then maybe—The woman begins to cautiously step around me. I've been in my head too long.

"Wait," I say.

"I said I'm sorry."

"No, it's okay. It's my fault. I should know better than to come up right behind someone when they received their iced coffee from the counter? Iced coffee? In February?" I stop when she laughs a little. I've made her laugh, and I mentally give myself a high five. Her laugh is breathy and light, housed by a full set of straight teeth. My adolescent self envies her. "Let me reimburse you." I bend for her cup on the floor where her name is spelled out. "Ava?"

She nods and feigns a smile as she looks up at me again—assessing me. I stiffen my lips as her eyes look me over, starting at my tapered fade and down to my chin. I take the napkin from her and blot it over my face in case any coffee landed somewhere only she can see. When I pull it back it's clean.

"Where exactly am I missing?" I circle my head with a finger. Ava blinks out of her head.

"Oh..." She laughs again. "No. Oh. Um. No, it's...you really..." Her sentence hangs.

Now things are getting awkwaaard. "I'm really...what?"

Ava clears her throat and points to her cup in my hand.

"Maybe I've had enough caffeine already."

I fake offense. "There's no such thing. I'll get you another."

She stops me with a hand on my arm. "No, you don't have to."

I look down on her, fluttering my eyelashes. "Please."

Her cheeks pinch and she lets go of my arm. "Iced caramel macchiato. If you must."

Caramel? I could have sworn I caught a scent of vanilla coming from her. I nod in answer and walk to the counter to request a reimbursement from Joe.

"What do you know," I lean over and whisper.

Joe shrugs. "Her name is Ava."

"You haven't seen her around before," I ask.

"Not before today."

"Alright, coo. Is she still waiting?"

Joe removes his wire rimmed glasses to wipe on his shirt before placing them back on his face, his eyes zipping over my shoulder and back. "Mhmm."

"Aye, gimme some," I say, with my fist extended.

"Take these instead." Joe hands over both mine and Ava's remade drink orders for the second time. "Knock em dead, Tiger."

"What?"

Joe shoos me away. I make my way back to Ava noticing Nugget at our table mouthing 'dibs,' his finger slicing across his throat. I ignore him and focus on Ava slow clapping as I make my way to her. She retrieves her refill from me and takes a sip.

"Delicious."

"Would you maybe—"

"Thanks again," she says and makes her way around the patrons sitting and standing around to leave the coffee shop.

Whoa, what?

When she's around the corner and gaining farther out of my sight, a need to see her again engulfs me. I don't want to buy her coffee, I want to buy her dinner.

My legs get the memo from my brain to move. I cut around the line to the table I was sharing with Nugget to stuff my laptop into my backpack and retrieve my coat from the back of the chair. Nugget's back erects.

"Cole, what are you doing? Cole. Cole, what are you—"

I give Nugget a wink and throw my backpack strap over my shoulder to run out of Bovaconti and for Ava.

When I'm out and on the other side of the glass window Nugget and I were plopped in front of I turn to him banging manically.

"I called 'dibs'," he yells around his hands cupped at his mouth.

I laugh and keep going. I catch her long braids making their way down Virginia Ave and yell her name. She stops and turns, while I shuffle through other pedestrians with my backpack caught in my coat, and cup of hot chocolate in my hand. I swallow my breath to keep from huffing in her face. Ava shivers in wait as I find the words to convince her to go out with me.

"So, a proper goodbye—or hello, isn't with coffee. How about dinner?" Her head tilts. "Will you have dinner with me?"

"You're asking me out?"

I smile and nod quickly—too quick? I stop and lean forward to hear her response. Ava doesn't expand her thoughts, she only stares back at me unamused. Fuck, she's wondering how to reject me. Our frigid breaths mix in the air between us. Her shoulders hitch closer to her ears and hugs her jacket. This wait is excruciating. I will my legs to leave and avoid anymore embarrassment, they don't listen.

"Are you sure you want to ask out a serial killer running from the law, eight kids in tow," she says.

Ha! She jokes. She's fun. I like a woman who I can laugh with...however, her face remains plain. She's making a joke right? I laugh as she continues to stare. I clear my throat and think of how to renege my invitation...respectfully.

"Are you—" She tilts her head to the side. "Ahh...Are you a serial killer with—with eight kids?"

The hustle and commotion around us mutes as I calculate if I can outrun her if she were to attack. Then Ava smiles wide and I let out a breath that could have killed me if she hadn't put me out of my misery. I smile with her before matching her dazzling laugh.

"You actually believed me," she says.

"A little," I say, still a bit unnerved. During that entire deliberation, she didn't blink once.

Ava catches her laugh. "Do you know the diner Heather's?"

I don't. "I'll find it," I assure her after being completely gullible.

"Mmk. Meet me there at 9 on—"

"Friday," I finish.

"All right. See you Friday at nine, Cole."

"Bye, Ava—" *Wait a minute.* "How do you know my name?"

She points to the cup in my hand with my name spelled out in black permanent marker. I laugh to myself as Ava keeps down Virginia Ave. Until Friday.

I walk off the elevator onto the sixth floor of Speck located on the outskirts of downtown Indianapolis, and situate myself at my cubicle, opening my laptop on my desk. Speck is a small publishing house which signs talent first. My boss and mentor, Matt, noticed my short stories I submitted throughout undergrad. Upon graduation, he offered me a cubicle and computer to continue providing content for the press. That was two years ago and my material is running low. Now, I'm tasked with a novel length manuscript. No matter the plot, no matter the characters, there's never a story.

And there will come a time pretty soon when my parents graduation gift in the form of five year's worth of rent will be ash and then I'll really be in trouble. Freelance editing and sporadic bar shifts will not cover housing, food, utilities, etc.

Last week I gave Matt a full manuscript. I wasn't extremely proud upon completion but my paranoia kicked in. It's unclear how much longer Matt will be able to keep me on without a novel. Short stories and poetry collections made Specks name in the beginning. Now, they have means to expand. I don't want to be left behind or cast aside.

I have been a wreck; seeking refuge in all-nighters at The Falcon with Nugget and Gail and then early mornings at Bovaconti. At least until a gorgeous woman spilled her coffee on me and accepted my dinner invitation. Remembering her humor, laugh and high cheekbones my fingertips don't leave my keyboard for the majority of the day. I'm writing a story, finally.

My computer chimes with a calendar alert from Matt requesting me in his office in ten minutes. Fuck. He's probably going to chew out the crap I turned into him last week. Never fear, I've started the new years best-seller.

I laugh to myself and my optimism I haven't felt in a long time, on my way to the printer and pick up my pages before heading into Matt's office where my last manuscript is atop his desk. I take the stack and throw it in his side trash can landing with an echoing thunk.

"Cole, what the—" His eyes shift from the bin to me as I perch on the edge of the seat in front of his desk. "What happened to your shirt?"

I rub my hand down my chest. "I met a woman."

"Ahh. And did you get her number?"

Shit. Why didn't I get her number, or her last name? "I got a date. Now, read this."

Matt looks to his trash bin and back to me, his chair creaking under his weight. He looks like The Rock's personal trainer without completing the extensive workout regimen. Some people are lucky, I guess—as I stand at six feet with thin arms and a bird chest regardless of how many chin ups I can accomplish. 40 in under 60 seconds as of last Thursday.

Matt clears his throat. "Although, I'm happy you did me the favor of trashing whatever you'd call..." He finishes his sentence with the wave of his hand around the trash. "It was complete crap and I—"

Ouch. "Yes, I know. This is new. First chapter." I drop the fresh pages, still warm from the printer, on his desk.

Matt relents under my unwavering stare, fastens his reading glasses on the bridge of his nose and gives me another chance.

Keeping my eyes glued to my lap, I wait.

"Cole."

I lift my gaze to a half smile. Good enough. I jump out of my seat with a clap. "Yes! Don't say anything. I'm going back to my desk. Gotta keep up the momentum."

"Send me updates," Matt calls on my way out.

The first place I go when I leave work is to my favorite Express to get my date outfit. Growing up, my parents would go all out for any occasion. I didn't need a new Lexus to drive my date to junior prom, especially since she snuck off with her senior ex; and I somehow ended up driving them to his house at the end of the night. I didn't need pork chops in a sack lunch or a king size bed in the third grade; there was never a limit when it came to them showing their unconditional love.

Now, I attempt to blend in with the basics; pack of white T-shirts, worn in shoes, and hand-me-down furniture. Which is another reason why being able to publish a novel is so important. Advances, royalties, building a following; I'd never have to work another bar shift and give my author career a real shot.

I adore my parents and the life they gave me except I always felt like they were making up for something beyond what I could ever ask for, when there was one thing I ever wanted.

"Someone's got a date."

Gail comes around the table of sweater vests I'm eyeing and shakes her head. Gail and Nugget used to date and paid their differences no mind, no matter the double takes. Gail as tall as a skyscraper, deep ebony skin tone; hand in hand with Nugget's shaggy red hair and wide frame of more than 200 lbs. Five years of off and on, got us all on the same page they should only be friends. And I get to keep them both for myself. She's in her final year of law school at IU Indianapolis and keeps her Express job to afford to look the part, and dress Nugget and I when we need a step above a shirt and overused jeans.

"Oh my God, Cole. What are you doing," she asks.

She's followed me to the nearest mirror where I'm holding up a red and purple checkered vest to my torso, trying to catch various angles. Gail snatches the clothing from my grasp.

"Let me do my job. Stay here," she orders, rolling her eyes as she stomps away.

She returns with the usual: white button up shirt and black slacks; dumping both in my arms and I grumble internally. I want to impress Ava. She deserves more than the usual.

I still can't pin down how she's captured me so. I have a craving to be near her again. After being with her for less than 30 minutes I've written over 10,000 words. She could probably be the source to bring out the best in my craft.

Chill. Out! I shout to myself.

"Follow me." Gail snaps me out of my head and I trail after the click clack of her high heels towards the register. Gail is one of few women in her class and is degraded by seemingly qual-ified and overbearing men trying to persuade her she should take up modeling instead before it's too late. She stands tall and talks clear to show she's not to be messed with.

I drop her offerings on the counter and wait for the total.

"What's her name," she asks.

Here we go. "Her name is Ava."

"Pretty?"

Oof, I press my hand to my chest to keep from falling off kilter, like when our eyes locked. Ava's golden toned skin, enhanced by her golden septum piercing; and full lips has my imagination running. "Ava is...she's one of those women who catches you off guard so you have to ask her out before someone else does."

"Like Nugget?"

"Oh, he tried."

Gail shakes her head, the bangs of her pixie cut batting against her eyelashes. "How do you know someone else hasn't already asked her out? I heard you didn't get her number. You could be yippy chi yay for nothing."

"Now you're starting to sound like him as well," I joke.

Gail slams her hands on the counter and I jump.

"Sorry," I say.

Even though Nugget and Gail have broken up and are better off as friends, it took Gail longer to realize. She takes a long breath to alleviate my fumble.

"Nugget may have rubbed off on me considering how long we've been together—er, I mean...been friends." The silence last as long as she stays in her head deliberating or reminiscing before shaking herself free. She continues, "Okay, your total will be ready once you get a new black tie."

"No, I need to get mine back from Nugget. He borrowed it for the—" I stop when Gail shakes her head. "Never mind."

"Be right back." I wait at the register as Gail goes to the display case and removes a black tie then returns to finish my transaction. I tap my credit card and accept my bag of clothes.

Gail calling on my way out, "Good luck on your date handsome. I can't wait for Nugget to tell me all about it."

Nugget's botched version won't compare to my first official date with Ava on Friday night.

After typing extensively throughout the day at Speck, I thought I could bring the adrenaline home. No such luck as I've been looking at the end of the same sentence for two hours. I know this story is more than 10,000 words. I feel the same way about Ava. She's more than spilled coffee and one date invite. She's—

My thoughts pause when I see Nugget's name across my phone screen. His relentless accusations start before I can say 'hello.'

"How could you Cole? You'd steal a woman from your best friend? You're a thief. How could you? How. Could. You?"

Is he done? "Are you done?"

He leaves me on the line for fifteen quiet seconds. "I'm done. She wasn't cute anyway and I'm sure I spotted cankles."

"Ava doesn't have cankles," I say, around a laugh.

"Ava," Nugget questions. "Sounds like a cankly broads name."

"It is the name of the woman who agreed to have dinner with me Friday night," I brag.

"Yea, yea. What else? I bet she has three kids and at least two ex-husbands."

I roll my eyes. "Why do you always have to go there?"

"If I don't who will?"

"Gail." Because they are two peas.

"Pssh. I'm more realistic."

The only thing real right now is how I feel about Ava. She's captivating, funny, creative; considering the faux story she pulled out of thin air—

"Hello?" Nugget breaks my reverie. "You're not falling in love already are you."

I scoff and hang up. No, I'm not falling in love with Ava. Ava and I are only meeting for dinner in three days.

CHAPTER 5
Ava

I'm running late for probably the 800th time in my life. Time moves too quickly and I've never been able to catch up. I stomp my foot into an untied Converse and run to open the front door on my way out. My shoelace catches under my foot and launches me into the hallway, into Casey's arms that push me back into the apartment, slamming the door behind him.

"Gah—" I flinch. It's too early in the morning for such animosity. I used to always be on guard when Casey and I lived together. It has been nice getting some carefree hours to myself. I also have to remember this is a brief arrangement. "What's up? Are you okay," I ask, tucking my shoelaces under my heel.

"Where are you going," Casey asks.

"I'm going to talk to Blaine. Do you want to come?"

Blaine doesn't preach about how 'you'll will be okay' or 'how special we are regardless of...' He listens to how we feel. We don't feel special. We don't feel okay. With Blaine's generosity and complimentary sessions, his help became welcome and appreciated.

"Nah. You know he and I never saw eye to eye."

Correction, Casey excluded, accepted Blaine's help.

I balance myself on the arm of the chair and tie my laces properly. "You know, Blaine still asks about you sometimes. I think he'd help you through what we're doing," I say.

"I don't want Blaine's help. I've never wanted anyone's help, Ava. I only wanted a family."

Blaine could never get through to Casey. He also has yet to give up. He doesn't see Casey as a challenge, he's worried about Casey's temper and how he's always holding his emotions inside.

Casey's defensiveness and hostility has always been pushed down, held beneath the surface. Knowing his family abandoned him, we're walking a fine line of destruction.

"I know, Casey...I'm saying he's helped me a lot. Blaine asks me the right questions and doesn't like to—"

"Blaine is your guy Ava, to deal with your problems. Don't try and make me one of them."

I lower my chin to my chest. "Okay. Never mind, I was trying to help. Forget it." I walk around him to make my way out.

"I'll think about it...okay," Casey says. I turn with an 'I told you so' grin and he rolls his eyes. "Go ahead, you're already late—I'm assuming."

One corner of Casey's mouth ticks up. I believe I'm forgiven for suggesting he do something he doesn't want to do, and I head off to see Blaine.

I can't keep my foot still while presiding across from Blaine, and for once it's not because of the sneakers skidding across the gym floor outside his office. I.e. nails on a chalkboard in my brain. Since there was little to no space at Miss Green's for over 20 children, Blaine received funding to lease a floor of a local building that has half a basketball court, lounge, and bar full of water and juices. It's a hub for the older kids to enjoy 3v3, do their homework, and enjoy a couple hours not being climbed on by the youngins, before loading back into Blaine's mini van to the foster home.

There's so much happening in my life right now: new apartment, new information affecting my best friend, and being away from Casey in general.

We've been side by side since we were three, when I entered a loud and cramped house full of strangers. I don't remember my life before Miss Green's or without Casey. He immediately took me under his wing; resulting in potential parents mistaking us as siblings, and being more than they'd bargained for.

Without Casey, I feel like I'm missing a limb. However, what I keep going back to is my Friday night date with Cole.

Cole looks exactly like Casey. I knew that from perusing his social media. I was struck dumb by their similarities...and their differences when I met him face to face. Cole's vibe is bright and buoyant, I want to bathe in it. He's the sandy beach to Casey's crisp autumn. Cole doesn't carry pain and resentment around with him, he didn't have to.

"Ava," Blaine starts.

"Hey, Dr. B."

"Again, I'm not a doctor," he says, in his casual attire of black rimmed eyeglasses, cropped sandy beard against pale skin and an untucked button up.

"Whatever." I shrug. Same song and dance, different play.

"What's new?"

"I have a date Friday."

"Where's Mitchell taking you," he asks.

I clench my fists. Do you ever get past someone who told you they love you one night to leave before the sun comes up? I haven't seen or heard from Mitchell at all.

Before Mitchell and I started dating, I'd see him all around the neighborhood—grocery shopping, along Monon Trail, art fairs. Did fate bring he and I to the same places at the same time or was he a Grade A stalker who had a plan to make me fall for him knowing it wouldn't last?

"I'm not with Mitchell anymore."

"I'm sorr—"

"Don't be," I snap.

"Do you want to talk about it," he asks.

I ponder with a long and loud hmm. Do I want to analyze why I let another man play me, leaving me dumbfounded and heartbroken? "No."

"Okay."

It's not like there's a way to know. For all intense and purposes, Mitchell has fallen off the face of the earth. It's unsolved, and I'll never get to know why—

"That asshole left my bedroom in the middle of the night and I haven't heard from him since," I explode.

"Were you expecting to?"

"It's common decency. He told me he loved me," I remember. "Mitchell held me a month ago, looked me in the eyes and said 'I love you so much, Ava.'"

"Did you say it back?"

"Yea, I said it...to myself," I say, backpedaling. "I would have told him in the morning." The fresh wave of humiliation has me kicking myself. I always say it first; and even when I don't, I end up abandoned. I'm not a love bomber. My word is my promise.

"Would you have meant it?" I give Blaine an obvious expression, he's known me long enough to know the answer. The only thing I am certain of is my heart—not so much my intuition.

"How did you...react waking up alone," Blaine asks.

No matter each failed attempt, I don't feel alone. It's my dream getting farther and farther out of reach I miss.

"I wasn't alone. Not really. Casey was there. He was there for me."

"Again."

I nod with a smile. The unconditional support Casey offers me...I love him. He's my best friend. "Casey will always be there for me."

"Why?"

I don't need to think. Me and Casey's friendship is the only thing I have to keep me going. "Because I'm always there for him...Casey has never needed me in the way I've needed him...Until now."

"What do you mean?"

I smile. "He helped me get a date."

CHAPTER 6
Ava

Our waitress places a cheeseburger and fries in front of Cole and a bowl of French onion soup with a side of fries in front of me. She huffs and puffs from whatever happened before we arrived. Cole and I can't keep our eyes off each other—each of us leaning into the table with matching bright smiles. Even with the out of date fluorescents and the smell of grease wafting from every nook and cranny, I'm only locked in on Cole.

"Anything else," she says.

I shake my head.

"No, thank you," he says.

We start into our dinner and Cole starts our conversation, "Do you live around here Ava?"

"Not a far walk." My reply is sharp.

"How'd you find this place?"

"I like to wander," I say, adding a heaping amount of ketchup to the side of my fries until the bottle sputters. I came across Heather's while walking home through a shitty rain storm and stopped for cover and nursed a plate of French fries for three hours until it passed.

"Mmm."

He's fighting for conversation. My answers aren't welcoming him into All Things Ava because this isn't about me and my goal of a three bedroom house tucked in a cul-de-sac.

I'm only here to get the answers Casey needs to…for closure? He hasn't revealed what he'll do with any information I'm able to gather. Closure sounds too easy. I'll have to keep watch to make sure whatever damaging intel I receive will not make Casey act out again.

When I bring my thoughts out of the impenetrable mind of my best friend, I notice Cole staring at me. Waiting for an answer?

"Sorry, what did you say?"

"I asked what you do—professionally," he says.

"Oh! I work at the Humane Society."

"Aye, there's the beautiful smile."

I didn't realize I was smiling.

"Vet tech?"

I refrain from snorting into my soup. It's…a sweet assumption. "Admin."

Cole doesn't break the wonder in his eyes. "You must like what you do."

"I love what I do." I reach into my bag and pull out the wallet sized photo I keep in my card holder. He takes it from me to look over. "I especially love this little guy. I named him Henry. Have you ever seen a fluffier St. Bernard?"

I smile at Cole looking at my pride and joy. Henry was surrendered at three weeks old on my second day of employment. I claimed him without a second thought regardless of the square feet of mine and Casey's rented bungalow. The last two years, I've scared away anyone who attempts to give Henry a double take.

I promised myself and Henry, I'd be the one who brings him home to a huge backyard and a family who'll treasure him as unconditionally as I do.

"Is he yours," Cole asks, returning the photo to me.

I tuck it back where it came from. "For the most part." Smiling at the future not too far off.

Cole holds my gaze; seemingly reading apart of me I haven't shown him. I hide in my bowl, my braids falling over my face, and dip a French fry in ketchup, into the French onion soup, and into my mouth.

"What the—" Cole's face is torn between disgust and curiosity.

My laugh hides behind my palm. "It's actually really good," I say behind a swallow.

His eyebrows have yet to relax. "Okay. Okay, what if their soup of the day was clam chowder?"

I shrug. "Would still be as good." I grab another couple fries, add ketchup and soup and hold it across the table. "Wanna try it?"

Cole covers his mouth and shakes his head. I don't let him off the hook so easily. I keep my arm extended and slowly...surely Cole drops his hands and resolve, takes a deep breath in and secures his lips around the fries and the tips of my fingers.

I pull back and lick the remainder of what Cole left behind. He's chewing quickly with his eyes closed. I dip, stir and eat more while Cole gets his bearings and opens one eye at a time.

"Good right," I say.

"Ack!" He grabs his water to squish around his mouth then swallows. "Absolutely not. Where did you come up with that?"

"Soup and frozen potatoes are economical. Gotta take what you get," I say.

Cole bites chunks out of his burger to mask the taste. He swallows and continues his inquisition. "Where did you grow up?"

"In foster care."

"Where?"

"Its been said I was passed around, maybe family, maybe not, until I ended up at Miss Green's foster care when I was three. Dirty and poor little orphan until I aged out. Now, I'm a dirt poor adult...orphan?"

"Oh...I'm sorry," he says.

Aren't they all. "Don't be, it's overrated."

"What is—"

"Born and raised in Indy then?" I clench my teeth. *Sense the tone, Cole.*

He clears his throat and follows my lead. "Indianapolis, yes. Downtown, no. My parents raised me near Midtown—" I tilt my head. "In Carmel, north of Indy. I plan to move back one day. They left me their house."

I keep my teeth together to avoid sputtering in amazement and jealousy that Cole has a house lined up for him whenever he's ready.

"Where did they go to retire," I ask with a drink of my water.

Cole drops his burger and suddenly can't seem to look me in the eye. Somethings changed. What's happened? If I had the chance, I'd never shut up about my family.

"My parents died last year, car accident," he says.

"Whac—" The water lodges in my throat with nowhere to go. My eyes tear and chest cramps. *His parents are dead?*

"Are you okay," Cole asks, gesturing around me, unsure how to help.

I punch my chest to clear my esophagus and release a proper swallow. I hold and relish the bit of air clearing my passages and take a deep breath in and out. "Dead? You said your parents are…" I can't repeat myself.

Cole nods his head. He can't repeat himself either.

"I'm sorry, Cole. I didn't know."

"Well, how would you," he says.

Fuck. "No, I don't—" I laugh longer than the moment allows. "I wouldn't. I didn't…I'm sorry."

Cole's responding smile falls too quick. I've lost my appetite and Cole lost his parents…Casey's parents.

What the hell am I doing? There's no information to gather. There's no family reunions scheduled to look Casey's parents in the eye and blame them for getting rid of one of their children.

Casey's plan has ended before it began. I can't get buried information. I don't want to do anything that'd bring more suffering to Cole. Behind a practiced facade is unresolved pain. One year isn't enough time to get over a parents death.

I need to be able to turn this night around. With little time to plan, I go with the first thing that comes to mind. Reaching across the table for his hand, he looks up to my mischievous smile.

"What?" His cheeks pinching.

"Follow me."

"Where—"

Catching him off guard, I intertwine our fingers and drag him out of our booth, through the diner and out the front door—our waitress yelling in our wake.

I pull Cole around two random corners to lose our tail in case we were being followed. Phew, the rush has me cackling; the windchill against my face, has tears leaking from the corner of my eyes. We stop at the corner when the walking sign has switched from white to red and I lean forward to catch my breath. I'm feeling much better about this night until Cole rips his hand out of mine.

My body shifts toward his back walking away from me.

"Hey, what's wrong," I ask, catching up.

"Ava, what the hell? What was—we left the diner without paying for our meal! And without our coats," he says, bunching his shoulders near his ears. Thankfully, Cole and I dressed in long sleeves, but it's still February, and night, and the Midwest.

"Yea, I know! What a rush." I raise my fists in the air. "Woo!"

He brings my arms down to my side. "Not 'woo.' It was illegal."

Okay... "You didn't feel anything—exhilarating? Not even a little? I mean, our conversation got heavy and I wanted to lighten the moment."

Cole wipes his hands down his face, one landing at his chin. "What—are we role playing again? Or are you simply crazy?"

I huff, dejected. I didn't make Cole smile, we're not having fun, and there's no way he's going to fall in love with me now. His parents are dead and he's calling me names. We're done.

I take a step back and raise my palms in surrender. "Okay. Bye, Cole."

"No—no." He catches my hand and doesn't let me go when I pull away.

No one has ever stopped me from leaving, I step into his chest by his tug. "I was only trying to lighten the mood," I say, eyes glued to the ground.

"By dine and dashing?" I can hear the smile in his voice.

When I look up, Cole's dark eyes are teasing me. We finally laugh.

"Maybe not one of my brightest ideas." My shaky hands wrap around his waist, the warmth coming off his chest sedating me. "I have a few more if you want to stick around." My bravery surprises me. It's easier to pretend with nothing to look forward to.

"Can I walk you home," he asks.

My arm stays hooked around his waist as we walk down the street huddled together as close as possible.

When we get to my apartment building, I hesitate with my keys because this will be goodbye. Goodbye to Cole and any information Casey thought I could obtain to comprehend why he grew up without a family.

"Thanks for walking me home, Cole," I say.

"It was the least I could do since I didn't pay for dinner."

We share a tense laugh.

"I had a good time tonight," I say, our final farewell.

Cole nods. "I'd like to take you out again and actually pay for our meals, if you'll let me."

I smile at the thought of seeing Cole again knowing it's impossible. He takes my smile as an invitation to close the gap between us. His eyes lower to my lips and I tilt my head away to keep him from coming any further. Before I know it, Cole's breath tickles my ear before his lips land on my cheek. Lips that ignite my body in a heat I'm all too familiar with.

"Okay, bye." I beep myself into my apartment building with my fob and take the stairs to the third floor and enter my home. My head falls into my hands, with my heart beating rapidly—

"Did you have fun tonight?"

I fall back into the door at the voice in my apartment. The living room lamp next to the couch clicks on and highlights Casey's silhouette.

"Casey—oh my God! What—wait, how did you—"

"Answer the question." He stands.

I swallow down my jumbled nerves. "I'm not uh...supposed to be having fun."

His long legs take two strides to stand over me. "You're supposed to be keeping up appearances!"

I almost bring my hands up to defend myself from his advance. "I am!"

I never yell back at Casey. He's my friend, not an attacker. Too bad tonight I'm tired and hungry, having not only ran out on the bill but my food too. Casey crosses his arms and I relax mine.

"I had a nice time. I think Cole liked me."

"You don't know anything yet."

Ugh. Casey goes back to the couch and I follow.

"Hello! Cole bought me dinner—er, planned on buying me dinner and that's something." God, who I am to defend a guy I met three days ago.

"Poor Ava," Casey says, stroking my cheek. "A free meal doesn't mean anything. This is why I'm here to help. I know how men work, I've seen them work you for an extremely long time—"

"Casey stop." I slap his hand away. "I get it."

I move to the opposite end of the couch and face away from Casey. He lets out an exasperated breath.

"Nothing against you, A. It's never been about the kind of person you are. It has always been about who they are," Casey attempts to reassure me.

"I know." I try to rub the sting in my nose away.

Casey doesn't say anything more. He gets up and heads for the door. I call for him when his hand is on the knob.

"Casey wait."

"Yea," he says, giving me his attention.

I stand and wipe my sweaty hands down my jeans. "Casey, your parents are dead. Cole told me tonight."

He nods. "I heard."

"When did you—"

"Anything else," he says.

"Everything else! I don't know about this. I don't want to see Cole anymore. You should have seen his face when he told me his parents are dead. It's too soon. He's still mourning."

"All the better. He'll be vulnerable and tell you what I need to know," Casey says.

"Uhm, you expect me to emotionally torture information about his recently dead parents?"

"Yes."

"Casey, that's evil!"

"No, it's necessary. How else am I supposed to get the answers I need?"

"You could always..."

He waits for me to come up with something we haven't already thought of and through before. I got nothing.

"This is how it has to be, Ava. You promised." His voice breaks on the end of his sentence. Our stares linger until he leaves my apartment.

Chapter 7
Casey

By some miracle, I made my way to Blaine's office. His back is relaxed and I'm rod straight, mentally calculating a variety of exit strategies. Through his office door, three flights of stairs and an eight minute jog back to my house. Or if worse comes to worse, throwing myself out the three story window.

"Casey, it's good to see you again," Blaine says.

I clench my teeth to keep from fleeing. I hate talking. I hate talking to professional talkers. "Ava suggested I come."

Blaine tilts his head. "How did her suggestion actually bring you to me?"

I shrug. I didn't call to let him know I was on my way. I showed up and he invited me in. Even though it is mid-afternoon on a Tuesday, the quiet seems too...quiet. Sterile. Suffocating. It's only me, the hum of the mini fridge and Blaine's thoracic breathing.

"Want to tell me about Ava's new guy?"

That grabs my attention. Blaine shouldn't know anything about Cole.

"What has she told you?"

"You helped her get a date. I didn't know you had other friends—"

"Cole is not my friend," I say, almost choking on my snarl.

"Well, where did you find Cole and how did you deem him best to date Ava?"

I cut my eyes away from Blaine and strategize how to make time pass. Showing up here was a mistake.

"Oh no," Blaine says.

I have to face him now. "What?"

"Don't tell me you found him on a dating app of some kind?"

I scoff. As if I'd ever set Ava up with someone more love sick than her who puts their name, age, and job on a dating site hoping for well suited prospects.

"I cannot wait for that fad to pass. It's pure laziness. Back in my day—"

Ah hell no, I don't have time for one of his ancient history stories. Blaine is at least 15 years older than me even though he might dress down. I clear my throat and Blaine stops his rant. I never thought he was capable of veering off topic. They say you learn something new everyday; I've learned Blaine has a high aversion to dating sites.

Blaine comes back to task and sits straighter, though not as straight as me. I'm usually hunched to hide except I don't like Blaine looking down on me...assuming me.

"How did you get Ava a date with a guy who is not your friend," he asks.

"Ava deserves to be happy," I admit.

I expect Ava deceiving Cole into falling for her, she'll gain the fearlessness she needs to prove to herself she doesn't need this dream of a partner and three bedroom house. Ava is beautiful, smart and undeniably lovable; any guy would be lucky to have her if she accepts herself.

"Is Cole a good guy?"

I huff. "I know for a fact Cole will not hurt Ava."

"You know who else hasn't hurt Ava," Blaine hints. "You."

I never have until...I yelled at Ava last night. I brought up her failed relationships and she almost cried. The memory has been wracking my brain since I left her apartment. My emotions regarding Cole cannot be what comes between Ava and myself. I need to think twice—thrice before reacting.

"I don't want to hurt Ava."

"Casey," Blaine says, leaning toward me. "Why haven't you stepped up to be the guy in Ava's life who doesn't hurt her?"

"Sometimes, Blaine, friendships are more important than the nuance of dating. I couldn't bear to lose her as a friend."

"Isn't it tough watching your friend get hurt time and time again—"

What about me! "I've been hurt too, Blaine," I spit.

He falls away from my outburst, registering the root of my anger. I mentally beg him not to bring up her name.

"Casey, do you want to talk about Rayv—"

No. Fuck!

The walls around me close in before he finishes her name. My heart swells and my breaths get shorter. The sides of my vision are cloudy and reaching the center, robbing me blind.

The memories flash in my minds eye. Years of what I thought was the greatest love I've ever received, Rayvin ruined my trust and my body. What she gave to me, she sold to others, resulting in the ongoing pain of my existence.

His bones crushing beneath my knuckles. Her screams. Then her nails against my back trying to pull me off him. The red and blue lights lighting up Miss Green's house like a Christmas tree. Ava crying in the corner.

"Casey. Casey. Listen to my voice. Breathe. Breathe with me."

The only thing I will give Blaine credit for is being able to draw me out of the dark place in my head. Whenever I've been overwhelmed to the point of devastation, Blaine's voice brings me out of the dark place Rayvin sends me into. I blink twice as the room comes back into view—few photo frames on the wall, gym bag in the corner, the smell of aged sweat seeping under the closed door. My eyes focus on Blaine, match his breathing, his hand covering mine on my chest. He must have gotten me on my back across the couch because above Blaine is the ceiling. I blink again.

"No." I swallow. "No, I don't want to talk about her."

"Do you want to talk about Ava?"

I groan as I bring myself up from the cushion. "Not if you're going to play matchmaker."

Blaine laughs under his breath and resumes his seat. "I'll play therapist then."

It's been two days since I saw Blaine and I barely get through my days; thinking I see her at the corner shop, the library, etc. I'm unable to sleep through the night. Rayvin haunts me.

I shouldn't feel this way. I never wanted to talk to Blaine, I knew he'd bring her up.

Rayvin Bell is the only person I'll ever love. Ten years of Ava re-reading fairy tales out loud about princes and princesses was foder until Rayvin. When she was admitted to our foster home, I saw past her split lip and swollen cheek, Rayvin only exuberated beauty. We shared our entire hearts and souls. Well, I did. There came a time when it wasn't reciprocated. And I haven't been the same.

My inner monologue has unconsciously brought me to Ava's apartment door and pounding for entry.

She opens the door and stumbles back as I barge in and pace the length of her living room. Even though I can hear her in the background, she's not Blaine. Ava doesn't have the influence to pull me out of my head. In my head, I'm 19 years old and alone, again. I'm always alone.

Ava steps in front of me and I barrel into her. I catch her by the forearms before either of us fall to the floor.

"Casey, what's wrong," she says.

"This is all your fault!"

I push Ava backwards. I wouldn't have known I did anything wrong if it weren't for Henry's loud bark followed by his low growl. Add that to the 140 pounds standing between Ava and I, I can finally reassess.

The only light on in Ava's apartment shines from the kitchen's oven light. Ava is dressed for bed; oversized T-shirt as pajamas, braids tucked inside her bonnet and eyes wide from my intrusion.

Ava pats Henry on the head and he relaxes in a squat but not a full sit.

I hang my head. "I'm sorry, are you okay?"

"I'm...confused. You wake me up in the middle of the night to yell and...you're becoming aggressive Casey. You pushed me and—"

"I said I'm sorry."

"And, if this continues, I will not be able to—"

"I went to see Blaine."

Ava stops. I needed her to stop. I didn't want to hear her finish.

"Oh…Great, right—and…?" What Blaine has given Ava, optimism; she always wished would rub off on me.

"I didn't talk about Rayvin." Ava nods. "I didn't want to talk about Rayvin.

"It was Blaine! He brought her up. And I haven't been able to sleep. When I do, it's for a short while and she's always there. It doesn't feel like a dream, it's like I'm reliving it all again. His face against my fist, her nails pulling me off him…it's been so long since…since I've been—it has been this bad, Ava." I hide my face behind my hands and breathe deeply.

"You were angry. I remember."

My hands slam to my side. "I was fucking tortured! I have never felt such pain before and you know I've been through it all. I hate her. I don't think I've ever mentally or emotionally come back from that day. I fucking hate her!"

Ava takes my hand. "I've felt the same way."

I snatch my hand from hers, swiping too close to her face and Henry growls. "No you haven't. Never bring her up again. Please!"

Her hands come up to protect herself and I lose my momentum. "Okay."

"And I can't go back to Blaine," I say.

Ava pulls me into her chest. My arms hang as she rubs circles into my back. "Do you want to spend the night with me?"

I sag deeper into her embrace. I've missed Ava. A lot. It's been the two of us all our lives and the past two months have been different without her, more than I would have expected. She's not around to tuck her cold feet under my legs or hog the television rewatching the black *Cinderella*.

However, between the two of us, Ava needs to keep focused. The life Cole had with his parents torments me daily. I need to know why, how.

"Not tonight." I step out of her arms and leave.

CHAPTER 8
Ava

After my first date with Cole consisting of dine and dashing and ending with me leaving him in the cold to fend for himself a way home; I thought I'd have to beg for a second chance. He sent me his phone number after reaching out to him on LinkedIn, and I called ready to apologize. However, Cole already had our second date planned. I clearly don't know how to get rid of men as well as they know how to get rid of me.

Cole asked to see me again the day before Valentine's Day. I said no. No matter my unyielding desire to be the one, I've always strayed away from all things Valentine's Day. I've never had a date nor creepy admirer, so I begged for Cole to let it be.

He stayed persistent with sweet and live texts watching the same movies I was binging on Lifetime, which resulted in me saying yes to my first Valentine's Day themed dinner.

Unlike our first date, Cole took me to an Italian restaurant in Fountain Square, where the silverware isn't wrapped in paper napkins. And the dining room is so quiet, I feel like I should whisper. Similar to our first date he's dressed in a white button up shirt, loose black tie around his neck and black pants—looking like our server; while I donned a cardigan over a white tank and cargo pants. I laugh to myself wondering if you dress the part do you get a discount of some sort.

"What's so funny?" Cole leans forward, antsy to be let in on the joke inside my head.

"You're dressed like the waiters here." I cover my laugh with my fingertips. "You could walk through the kitchen and get a free meal if you didn't find free restaurant food illegal."

He returns my smirk. "Am I so transparent?"

"What do you mean?"

Our waiter comes back with our appetizers. Cole motions for me to go in first. I go for show, snapping my napkin in front of me before placing it on my lap, then use my fork to slice into a ball of arancini. After the first bite, I'm falling back into my chair. The question Cole didn't answer forgotten.

There's a difference between survival and living. Casey and I have had to survive with an awfully strict budget and cashing in recyclables. Cole has lived his life with the inclination hard work and dedication would guarantee him anything he's ever wanted. There's not a moan or an exaggerated eye flutter escaping him from our appetizers. He must have grown up with more seasonings than salt, pepper and expired garlic powder because *this* is the best food I've ever tasted.

I savor each bite throughout my first Valentine's Day dinner until I can barely pick up my fork. My chews and movements get slower and slower, my determination pushing me not to waste half my meal.

"We can get a to-go box, Ava."

"No, it's okay. I can finish it. I uh—phew, give me a moment." I try to breathe through the pang of my pants button digging into my abdomen.

"You're full," Cole says.

My hand shakes trying to bring my fork to my mouth again. I feel like if I eat another bite, I'll vomit. Against my entire life's existence, I surrender and drop my silverware. "Who knew places served such large amounts of food. I hate I can't eat another bite, there's so much left."

"It won't go to waste," he says.

There's no more strength I'm able to stretch beyond my ears and sense of intrigue. Our waiter returns and Cole gives him his credit card to run. He didn't even look at the check! What the hell—oof, I place a hand over my gorged belly and focus on steady breaths when our waiter returns Cole's card and receipt. He boxes the rest of my dinner as he signs.

"There's no way I'll be able to finish this," I whisper. I'll be full for the foreseeable future and I don't want to bring it home to rot.

Cole smiles at me and my belly full of the best Italian I've ever had mixes with butterflies. Cole is entirely too handsome. Chiseled features, attentive eyes, an aura of care. How is he single? How am I the person he'd call three times to ask on a date?

"Follow me," he says.

Cole rounds the table and offers his hand. I accept, stand, then follow him through the restaurant with my to-go box tucked under my arm.

He pushes his way through the double doors to the kitchen and my grip hardens to stay close to him; as well as, to avoid getting lost in the hustle behind the scenes.

The kitchen must be sound proof because it's pure chaos back here. Pans colliding, cooks yelling for servers, etc.

In the back corner, a pastry chef is setting three plates with pieces of tiramisu.

"For me right," Cole asks.

He stands and gives Cole a once over, unsure. I stand behind him to hide. This is not the way to steal from restaurants. Too much time is passing for the emergency button to be pushed and the cops to show up.

The pastry chef turns and boxes the small dessert.

"Can I get a bag," Cole says.

He then reaches under his silver table covered in sugar and spice to produce a brown paper bag. Cole takes the bag, places my to-go box in the bottom and the dessert on top.

"Thanks."

"No problem..."

Cole takes my hand again and leads me through the back door. We step into the crisp night and as soon as the door closes behind us—

"Cole, what the hell," I say, whipping my hand from his.

"Not yet," he says, slinging his arm across my shoulders.

What?! Cole called me crazy when I pulled him through the diner last week. He can take a free dessert without any consequences and—

"This way." His arm travels down my back, his hand landing at my waist, pulling me against him.

I don't waver even though my cheeks heat as were pressed closer. Where the hell are we going and who the hell does Cole think he is? Berating me for dine and dashing one day to steal food the—

"George?"

Who the hell is George? My internal fuming landed us in front of an older, unhoused gentlemen sprawled out on the street against a brick wall.

"Ugh, you again. What now," George says. His russet brown skin tone is eclipsed by his dirty coat, dirty nails, and bad attitude. He's unshaven, unbathed and his grimace intensifies by his uninvited guests.

Cole kneels to make eye contact with George. If I can smell the amount of time George hasn't had a shower from standing in front of him, I can't imagine all Cole is able to sniff right in front of his face. He opens the bag of leftovers and fresh dessert, bringing out the pastry first. George snatches the box from Cole then tucks the bag to his side.

"Keep walking, Cole."

Cole stands, entwines our fingers and we do as told. Cole pulls me along, my confusion guiding my head to look behind me where George has a handful of chocolate ladyfingers.

"Soooo, you dress as a waiter to get free food from kitchens to give to the homeless." Cole shrugs. "What—who are you, Robin Hood?" Cole laughs at my lame joke without answering. "No, seriously. I'm not asking why—I'm wondering...I guess I'm wondering how you know George?"

"Well first, I didn't steal," he says.

My hand acts on its own accord and crushes his in mine. "Did you pay?"

"No—"

"Steal!"

"No, Ava. The owners are family friends. It's not a big deal."

"Likely story. You expect me to believe that."

Cole shrugs. "Up to you. And second, you saw George. Saw how angry and put off he is?"

"Yes, intimidatingly so."

"And when you turned around I'm sure you saw his smile with a mouthful of dessert," Cole says.

"I did." A cherry on top of an intimidating cake. George likes food not people. I can respect that.

"I don't know what George has been through to be where he is now. I know he used to yell at people who'd walk on 'his street.' There came a time, I felt like I was having just as bad a day, I wasn't. I couldn't have. However, I thought, why not? And I joined him in his screams. Sometimes it feels good to scream, ya know?"

Not at Miss Green's. You can't scream a bad day away—or at all, in a foster home. That's how rumors start. Neighbors like to pretend to be a good samaritan without doing the work to limit crowded homes. We all had to find different coping mechanisms for self-loathing and impending failure. Me, romance books.

"I yelled for a while. George screamed for longer. As he continued, I got hungry. He was the best company I had that afternoon so I went to get us sandwiches. Mid-yell at a woman walking her dog, George took the extra sandwich from my hand, before I even offered it to him, might I add. As the distressing volume of the world continued, George and I found a bubble of silence eating BLT"s. Am I dying to know his life story? Of course. He's missing a thumb!

"I figure it's the least I can do, if food abates whatever activates his fits of rage."

Wow. Cole took it upon himself to feed George, without knowing how it'd benefit the people of Virginia Ave, to keep him from yelling at people in the street. It's no cure for cancer but I'd bet people saw brighter days.

"That is remarkable, Cole."

He showed me a piece of his heart and I'm mush. Curse this holiday with their acts of service and gifts. I stem my awe because it's too soon to think Cole is anyone better than who raised him.

"Don't act like I'm the only one trying to make a difference," he says.

I rack my brain before looking up at him. How the hell could I possibly be making a difference for people in the world? People—most people are horrible. I'm with George there.

"Your advocacy for animals," he says.

Oh. Well who wouldn't? You don't have to lie to an animal to love you, they come predisposed. Animals are simply better than humans. I don't know if Cole knows what he's getting himself into saving one person at a time, considering he's the offspring of Mr. and Mrs. Evil; and it's not up to me to ground him.

"So, you'll help the animals and I'll help the people. Thus we single handedly save the entire world," he says.

Cole Roberts, what a dreamer.

CHAPTER 9
Ava

It's Sunday afternoon. And I've ordered enough food for lunch and dinner to have leftovers for tomorrow's breakfast—my appetite came back quicker than I thought from the previous nights feast. I've been couch ridden, huddled in a blanket under my sweatpants, and binging the Lifetime Movie Network all day.

No matter my dating status, I do not get exhaustingly sad or bitter by romantic comedies.

The high-powered CEO having to choose between the barista with a fascination for Italian paintings versus the yacht mogul. Tell me more.

Oh! She can't start her day without a latte and has fond memories of her family spending summer days on their boat? Yes, and?

And the barista wants to cater to her need to travel, while the mogul wants to park the boat and party. The answer seems obvious to me while she keeps me on the edge of my seat, mentally. Physically, I feel myself sinking further into the couch.

The buzzer to my apartment goes off right before she's about to make the ultimate decision to change her life. I turn up the volume to ignore the buzzer sounding once, twice and then nonstop as whoever lays on it without coming off.

I fight out of my covers and go to the intercom.

"Yes," I huff.

"Delivery," says a gruff voice.

Hmm. I haven't ordered more food. Or have I? I allow him to enter and wait in the hallway.

I look past the man coming off the elevator with a bouquet of flowers.

"Ava?"

I slit my eyes at him, down the empty hall, and back to him.

"Ava who?"

He looks to the card poking out from the bouquet. "Ava from Cole?"

Cole got me flowers? I come up off the door and reach my arms out to receive the monstrosity of purple roses. The apartment door closes behind me as I set the vase on the dining table.

I read Cole's note:

Thank you for being my date yesterday. Be mine, today.

Cole

Holy hell. Boy's got game.

I'm fanning myself with Cole's note when I notice the credits are playing. I don't know if the CEO chose the coffee or yacht guy. Cole choosing me makes her decision irrelevant.

Best Valentine's Day ever.

Chapter 10

Casey

Two dates in less than 24 hours? If I didn't know any better I'd say my twin brother is as desperate as my former roommate.

Ava has been in a number of relationships and no matter what she's tried, nothing ever bred different results. Always donning a pair of rose colored glasses. Even now, she's laughing and can't keep from flipping her hair.

I don't know why women's magazines suggest flipping their hair guarantees a man's attention, least of all at dinner. Ava should be eating her braids as they land every which way.

I will give her credit for holding back affection. Cole will take her hand or hold her under his arm but there's nothing else to show for it. I've seen Ava physically invested and it's not with Cole. She'd be on him like white on rice, if this wasn't fake. Ava keeping her physical distance allows me credence she won't fall for whatever sweet nothings coming out of his mouth.

Cole and I look the part to attract a woman: straight teeth, standing height at 6'0; unlike me, Cole's aura gets him successfully farther than I ever have—open, kind, unscathed. Unless you consider Rayvin. And I don't, not anymore.

No one could deny what Rayvin and I felt for each other was real. However, real feelings do not diminish unforgivable actions. Four years of soft kisses and warm embraces couldn't recoup what she did.

Relationships only appear effortless. Two people laughing. Two people holding hands, kissing. No one ever looks at one person at a time. I do.

Ava and Cole are laughing and seemingly enjoying each other's company. Cole's smile stretches and I never knew Ava to be funnier than the 7 ate 9 joke.

However, Ava is leaning away from the table, even while eating. A tell tale sign she's doing her best to avoid the romantic spell Cole is trying to put her under for their Valentine's Day date and he's too punch drunk to notice.

He lays his palm facing up on their table, waiting for her to attach them. While Ava keeps her extra hand in her lap. Cole's conviction battles her insistence.

I've always been invested in the men in Ava's life. She's a dreamer and optimistic of good people—or a good person—to bring her out of her sport of make believe. She puts so much pressure on what she thinks her once upon a time should be instead of what they are—two different people figuring out how to share one life together.

Ava has pursued anyone battling a bad habit. Though slow to admit, she attaches herself to people like her birth mom. Gambling their life away with their choice of poison. Freud, back at it again.

This is my first Valentine's Day without company in 18 years. The three years before being admitted to Miss Green's were inconceivable: I was unwashed, shit stained, and hungry. I shouldn't be able to remember those years, Ava doesn't. Only I do. I had Ava on this holiday both of us refused to celebrate. This year I have no one. I've always been by myself, with or without Ava; this year feels different.

I never thought there was a chance Ava and I would be apart as life has kept us close. Still, one day, someone—not Cole, will be the man for her and she'll move on without me.

Worst Valentine's Day ever.

CHAPTER 11
Cole

"EVERYBODDDDYYYY LISTEN!"

"Oh my God." I hide under my hand while Nugget is standing on the bar top, tequila shot in the air, all eyes on him.

"My best friend—NAY! My brother—has graced the world with his presence for 26 years today. Please follow me in raising your glass." Slowly the bar patrons raise whatever they're drinking. "To Cole!"

"To Cole," Gail yells.

"To...Cole," the bar litters around.

Glasses come together with their closest neighbor—some more energetic than others. Nugget has been trying to get through his toast the last three minutes and one thing he's right about is my age. I am 26 years old.

Nugget wins women over with his humor, he won me over with his loyalty. This past year especially, he's been there for me. I didn't need to call or wallow extensively. Nugget knew exactly when to come around.

"All right, down," Sarah says, swatting his legs with a dish towel from behind the bar.

Nugget makes his way back to the ground without spilling a drop, knocks his shot glass to mine and we take it at the same time.

"I love you, man," I say, bringing him in for a bear hug.

"Down boy," Gail says, pulling us apart. "Cole is taken." It's her turn to hug me. "And happy birthday."

"Thanks Gail."

"If he's so 'taken'—where is she," Nugget says. "I've only barely saw her once. Wait, no. More like nonce."

Gail and I share a look. "Boy, what," she says.

"Not once," Nugget clarifies. Then they both face me crossing their arms.

I stiffen. I've always made a huge deal about my birthday. Growing up, I made sure everyone knew I'm on another trip around the sun. The parties my parents threw me? Unmatched. Exotic animals, renting out an ice skating rink, hotel suites. My classmates anticipated invitations months in advance. My birthday is the only day I wouldn't bitch when my parents went above and beyond. Because the celebration always ended with a cake and a wish. And I always had the same one.

Since my parents deaths, and my limited funds, The Falcon has been helpful and accommodating—perks of renting one of their studios upstairs and picking up bar shifts. A week at the office and the ebbs and flows of writing a manuscript; half off spirits in the middle of the day is a no brainer.

Ava, on the other hand, is the complete opposite of a no brainer. She wrecks my brain constantly. I can't help feeling like she's yanking me along. And I can't help refusing to cut the cord. I'm trying to leave myself a smidge of dignity, which is why I didn't mention my birthday to her.

"I didn't tell Ava it's my birthday," I say.

"What," Gail and Nugget exclaim.

"Whoa, what does this mean," Gail says.

I shrug. "We're still new. Taking our time getting to know each other. I don't want her to see me fucking lit or whatever."

"Pssh," Nugget rags, taking his bottle of Stella to the head, then releases a long belch. Sounds like you're blocking yourself."

"Wha—I'm not blocking myself. I'm...I'll call her. The least she can do is wish me a happy birthday." I finish my Stella for liquid courage—this could either go really well (her running to The Falcon to wrap her arms around my neck in birthday glee) or really bad (I throw up with her on the phone from nerves). I put my empty bottle on the bar and retrieve my phone from my back pocket, Ava's contact being the third one listed in my recents.

I press the phone to my ear and wait out the rings to unite Ava and I.

"Hello," she answers. I freeze. We may have only started getting to know one another but something I caught on to quick is Ava will either answer as soon as possible or hours later. "Hello, Cole?"

"Happy birthday!"

Nugget mirrors my hand to the forehead and Gail twirls a finger to Sarah indicating another round of tequila shots.

"How'd you know," Ava says.

"Uh know what?"

Know what, mouth Gail and Nugget.

"It's my birthday...almost. Tomorrow I'll be 26," Ava says.

"I'm 26 today." My friends nod, following along to one half of the conversation. "Wow, you make it hard not to think about you."

Nugget turns his back to me and wraps his arms around himself, his hands coming up and down his back—insinuating an aggressive make out. Gail fails to get his arms to his sides.

I hear her breath catch and I smile to myself. As much as Ava continues to excite me, I'm happy to know I also have an effect on her.

"Happy birthday, Ava."

"Thank you, Cole. Happy birthday to you."

"Can I see you tomorrow? Treat you to a birthday dinner?"

Gail and Nugget both give me a thumbs up for approval. I turn my back to them and plug my other ear to ignore their snickering. I should have made this call in the bathroom.

"That'd be nice. Let's narrow down details tomorrow?"

"Tomorrow? Can you tell I'm up to no good today?"

She laughs. "There's not much you'll be able to keep from me, Cole."

Ava from beginning to end: mystery and intrigue.

"You're the easiest girl I've ever dated," I say.

"I'm sorr—What?"

Shit. I immediately know she misunderstood based on the twin smacks against the back of my head from my friends. I squeeze my eyes shut to turn back time. How did my emotional confession make me out as a hormonal jerk?

"No, no, I'm sorry—I meant you're a girl—woman I'm dating, whom I like. I like a lot," I clarify and cross my fingers as the pause lingers. "Better?"

"I like you too, Cole," she says.

I lift one fist in the air. "Please answer my phone call tomorrow. Not tonight, no matter what. Tomorrow, okay?"

"Okay. Enjoy the rest of your birthday."

"Thanks Ava, I'll—"

And she's gone. For the better, so I don't embarrass myself further.

CHAPTER 12
Ava

Cole and I see a lot of each other in the upcoming months. We go to the movies, museums, parks and enough dinners too make me consider adding weights to my ankles and a waist trimmer to my stomach. I've never considered myself in shape and I walk 90% of the time but considering the calories and amount of foods Cole and I venture, I can at least try to keep my present figure.

With all our time together, finding out Cole is ambidextrous, allergic to cats, and beautifully humble; it's not the information Casey is looking for. They share the same genes. However, Cole is allergic to fish, while Casey is a sucker for all you can eat sushi.

Cole's characteristics are not what matters to Casey. Casey needs to know about his parents. He needs to know why they left him and kept Cole. What happened after his first couple minutes of life that was so threatening to Toni and Shawn they refused to take him home?

I'm playing the part of adoring girlfriend: holding hands, talking on the phone until one of us falls asleep, learning more about his craft; without crossing the line physically—intimately. He's only gotten as far as my apartment building and I always have my key ready to let myself in and keep him out. Cole is putting his best foot forward while I am forming questions for intel on Toni and Shawn Roberts.

Spending all this time with Cole in any other environment would be rewarding if his parents weren't incarnated from Satan. Cole makes me question nature versus nurture. How or why is he all good?

"Ava—" Blaine snaps his fingers in front of my face. "Come back, please. Staring off into space doesn't help pay my bills."

"I don't help pay your bills, Blaine."

He nods. "I assume you'd like to talk about Cole more—first is there anything you'd like to talk about outside of your perfect boyfriend?"

Boyfriend? "Blaine! If Cole hasn't called me his girlfriend you can't call him my boyfriend." I am aware of my time and place and I can't have Blaine putting labels where they don't belong. Even though...it's clear as day, Cole would make the perfect boyfriend. Except even the perfect boyfriend wouldn't forgive me for conning him.

"Well, there's not much I don't know about Cole...except his favorite color."

"Green."

Blaine and I smile together. My smile teetering on a crush and betrayal. Casey is going to kill me.

Cole meets me on the street of Blaine's building. Since he was in the area for lunch, he stopped to walk me back to work. And I get the chance to introduce him to my extra special someone. Even though Cole has been putting in the time and consideration to make me feel like the only woman in his world, he isn't the only man in mine.

To avoid questions I'm not prepared to answer, I told him I'm a Big Sister. I'm not sure when exactly you should tell your temporary significant other you talk to a semi-licensed professional to trauma dump abandonment and man drama. Two months seems too soon. Plus this isn't about me, it's about—

"PENIS!"

I hold my hands over my ears. "What the—why are you screaming 'penis'?"

"Needed a way to get you to come back to me. You're always in your head," he says.

I drop my hands. "I'm here."

Cole tucks me under his arm, shielding me from the harsh winds smacking us in the face. The sun is out. Not low. April is here. Spring is not. And since I have yet to sneak back into Heather's for my coat, I've had to improvise with never enough layers. I tuck my hand in my sleeve and breathe into it for warmth, locking into the present.

"Where is...the farthest you've gone," I ask.

"Uhm...excuse me?"

"Where's the farthest you've ever gone?"

"I know, like...you mean as in with my first girlfriend or—"

I shove myself out of his grasp. "What, no! I meant traveling."

"Oh." He holds a closed fist over his mouth to clear his throat. "Mmm, my parents took me to Iceland when I graduated high school."

I fight to keep my eyes still. It's not his fault. "I meant in Indiana." I didn't actually. I don't want to hear about his extravagant international vacations with his family.

"My parents and I would go to the dunes often. Definitely holds my favorite memories."

"The dunes?" I think I remember reading about that place. I wrack my brain, and I realize it was in Palm Springs...California. I give up. "Mmm, how long is the plane ride?"

He laughs into my hair, I didn't notice when we came back together in embrace. "You don't need a plane to get to the dunes, it's like a beach about three hours north."

Uhm, there are few stories based in Indiana and none of them have ever mentioned a beach. I call bullshit.

"Okay well I've never been on a plane or the Dunes Beach."

"Bae—" *Bae?* "It's just the dunes—Indiana Dunes."

Whatever. "I'll be sure to put it on my bucket list."

"Never say never," he says.

"I didn't say never."

Cole leans his head on top of mine. "It's an expression."

Cole clamps my hand as we walk through the various aisles of all the different dog breeds held at the humane society up for adoption. In a perfect world, I'd live on 100 acres of land and take in abandoned or surrendered dogs to raise as my own. Per usual, my salary puts a dent in my dreams.

We walk up to Henry's cage and I'm instantly flooded by an unconditional affection for him. No matter if I bring him to my apartment for a night or a week to bring him back here, Henry is my dog—and the beginning of my family.

When Henry sees me, he shakes his tail before sitting. I open his cage and kneel to embrace all 140 pounds of him in my arms. From experience, it's better to meet him in the middle to avoid being plowed over.

Cole clears his throat, interrupting the kissy noises I'm making in Henry's ear in greeting. I give him one more for good measure then stand, my hand still massaging the top of his head.

"Henry, someone is here to see you," I say

When Henry advances to sniff him out, Cole presses himself against the wall.

"Henry wait." My dog stops. "Are you okay Cole?"

"Uhm. He uhm…Henry looked like a puppy in the photo you showed me," he says.

I snap a leash to Henry's collar. "He definitely plays like one." Cole doesn't let up from the wall. We both take a step back. "You can pet him if you like."

His forehead begins to perspire. "I thought he was a puppy. You know smaller."

I fight to hold in my laugh. "They were all puppies before Cole. Follow me back to my desk." He nods without coming off the wall. "Five steps behind, for your safety." I give him a teasing wink.

Back at my desk, Cole is looking over the both of us from the other side, while Henry relaxes at my feet. His loud huff and big roll to lay as close to me as possible makes my heart swell.

"What's his story," Cole asks.

"Henry was surrendered at six weeks old. Did you know dogs aren't even supposed to leave their mother before eight weeks? Unfortunately, she didn't make it. His mother died after birthing her litter. Henry came in three days after I started working here. If I ever were to believe in fate..."

Henry shifts, pushing me farther from my desk. Cole jumps back. I don't laugh this time. Considering Henry's size it could take some getting used to if you didn't watch him grow up from three pounds to 140lbs.

"He's not what I expected," Cole says.

"I know, you thought he'd be smaller." I hold my lips together to hide my amusement.

"I'm not scared! I want to make that clear, he's umm—"

I pull open my desk drawer and pull out a dog treat. Henry, attuned to my movements, bolts up and sits.

"Here." I offer the treat to Cole. Hesitantly, he creeps around and accepts the gift.

Henry's gaze volleys between Cole and I. Slowly, I guide Cole's hand to the waiting St. Bernard. Henry laps the treat in one go.

"Tickles," Cole says and I feel like I'm allowed to laugh again. I give him a Clorox wipe to remove Henry's slobber from his palm.

"I can't wait to take him h-o-m-e soon," I say.

"Home," Cole asks.

Henry barks out loud twice then hops into my lap, testing the weight of my desk chair, and licks my cheeks.

"Ah, oh my god. Henry down." My smart boy climbs off and rests on his haunches. I give him another treat. "Now you know why I had to spell it out."

"Did you teach him that?"

"Not at all. He's just a smart cookie." Henry barks. "Crap—" I give him another snack. "He knows h-o-m-e either means I'm leaving or he's coming with me. I feel kinda bad hauling him back and forth."

"What's stopping you?"

"Er, from?"

"From taking Henry ho—"

I cough loudly into my fist and shake my head.

"H-o-m-e." Cole smiles.

"Ha, oh. I don't have one to give him. Henry deserves a h-o-u-s-e." Cole gives me a look and I shrug playfully. "Didn't want to chance it. Henry deserves a family to play with, and a dog park...my apartment and the patch of grass on the corner isn't going to cut it." I give Henry a deep scratch. "We'll get there."

"Yea, I know you will," Cole says.

I keep my head down, absorbing Cole's belief in me. When I look up, I notice his sincere words accompanied with his honest eyes. God, he's amazing.

I gave Cole a part of me today. Henry has been the one thing I've ever gotten to call mine. With Henry, I see a plan and dream for my future. My St. Bernard. My hope.

Speaking of hope, I hope Cole falls for me before I completely fall for him.

CHAPTER 13
Cole

I walk into The Falcon and see Nugget by himself at the bar. When I take the stool to his left he chokes back his beer when he sees me.

"Dude, where have you been," he asks.

"Ah man. I've been with Ava." Even saying her name out loud brings a smile to my face. Nugget rolls his eyes and I shove him. "What have you been up to?"

I raise my hand to attract Sarah. She looks my way and nods.

"Since you've been hanging out with Ava, I've been hanging out with Gail," Nugget says.

God dammit. Nugget and Gail: better off as friends, insane physical attraction, shouldn't be left together too often. "Nugget, no!"

Nugget fakes nonchalant with his hand pressed to his chest. "What could you possibly mean by 'Nugget, no?'"

Sarah sets an open Stella in front of me, I smile at her in thanks. "Don't play coy. Every time I like someone you go right back to Gail."

"We're friends."

"Then be her friend," I say.

"That's what I said."

"*Do* what I said, Braxton Edward Yoakum."

Nugget blinks a few times. "Damn. Okay dude."

Using his entire name tells him I'm serious. We've been on a two year streak of mutual friends and I'd like to keep it going.

"Tequila," Gail says.

She falls in the stool on the other side of Nugget with an exasperated breath and we bounce apart. We ended up in each others space trying to emphasize our points. I adjust to the back of my seat as Gail slams the shot glass on the bar, un-buttons her shirt to replace with a Butler hoodie. Sarah starts pouring her another shot along with setting three new Stella's on the bar—she's too good to us.

"What kind of friends are y'all to have started without me," Gail says.

I look at our full bottles of Stella. "It's not like we're cele-brating."

Gail takes three gulps of her bottle. "Who cares? Make something up. It's been a long day." She swallows her second shot in less than two minutes without flinching.

"You okay hun," Nugget asks.

Gail and I turn to Nugget with accusing eyes. He might have been at The Falcon longer than I thought. Drunk lips, truth slips.

Nugget tries to laugh it off. "Not hun like hunny. I mean, hun like HUNRGH." He mimics a wrestlers stance after body slamming their opponent. "You know?"

It gets worse when he pats the top of Gail's head.

She swats him away. "Boy. Now, you know better," she says, smoothing her hair back in place.

I close my eyes and take my Stella back full force. "You good though," I ask her.

She takes three long pulls from her bottle. "Nothing I can't handle." Her burp lasts seconds. "Tomorrow."

"Hot," Nugget says, catching his side from my elbow knocking into him. I need to schedule a guys night asap.

"Writing going well," Gail asks me.

"Ugh, maybe tomorrow," I reply, wiping my hands up and down my face in turmoil.

"Mmm. And Sarah told me they're out of pretzel bites," Nugget chimes in. Gail and I wait for him to explain how his point and our funk correlate. "I guess we all got problems. Am I right?"

"Boy—"

"Hey Sarah!" Nugget wiggles three fingers when she gives him her attention. With three shot glasses full of tequila,

Nugget grabs the middle one and me and Gail follow his lead.

"To tomorrow," he says.

CHAPTER 14
Cole

With all the time I've been enjoying spending with Ava, I've completely ignored my manuscript. When I add anything, it's crap and Matt doesn't have a problem letting me know. I'm wasting everyone's time. Considering I feel my time with Ava is limited, I can at least keep my job.

I started this manuscript on an impulse driven by getting a date with an intriguing woman, and all the good stuff came out at once. As I'm now dating the intriguing woman, the rest of my story is getting complicated. Whenever Ava prevents me from going into her building, or kissing her goodnight, my nerve in all things plummets.

I know I have something special with this story, like I know I have something special with Ava. And they both happen to be quite stubborn.

To make matters worse, my lunch date this afternoon is with Matt. A free lunch is usually a good bet, if only it didn't guarantee termination of employment. When you're at a job long enough you notice cues with the higher ups. Matt's cue is inviting you to a lunch at Ruth's Chris on his dime before he gives you the boot.

I've never been remotely close to a free lunch with Matt until this project. I've avoided his prior check ins with me slipping by with an appointment excuse until I couldn't think of another way out. Maybe with back to back doctor appointments, Matt will think I'm sick. And you can't fire a sick person, it's immoral.

Our waiter places a cheeseburger and fries in front of me and steak with mash potatoes and gravy in front of Matt. I push my plate away an inch knowing I won't be able to keep anything down.

I'd rather the Tom from Marketing treatment: he sends you an e-mail, you have until the end of the day to pack up and leave. No muss. No fuss.

Matt is enjoying his meal too much for someone who's about to give me the worst news of my career. I'm mentally Googling careers after losing my dream job and the best I can come up with involves a mop and bucket. Tomorrow sucks.

I can't keep in my disgruntled irritability any longer— "Am I getting fired?"

Matt looks up at me from his plate. I planned to be calm and give Matt a logical explanation on my skillset and work ethic to convince him to keep me on, before the thought of a jumpsuit, bucket and floors that never get clean took hold of my consciousness, which took hold of my mouth.

Matt swallows a mouthful of steak and potatoes then looks at me with solemn eyes.

Oh no. "Before you say anything, let me explain. I started *Because of Her* on a whim and now that whim has become important to me. Our stor—this story is important. Really, really important Matt. I'm going to finish it. I promise. I need more time. Please."

My ramble leaves me parched. I reach for my ice water and chug to its base.

Matt sets his silverware on the table, and hunches his massive shoulders. "Oh no, Cole. You love her."

His statement takes me by surprise. So much surprise I spit my water across the table. I'm frozen until he brings his napkin from his lap to blot his shirt. Thanks to our late lunch, the dining room isn't full. My shame doesn't stretch further than our table. Fuck, I'm definitely fired now. "Matt, I am so—"

He raises his massive palm to shush me. "As I was saying, the way you know about my lunches, I know about your writing technique. Courting a woman produces your best work. Then when you love her—"

"Nah, I don't think—"

I stop when Matt raises a palm the size of my face. "When you have decided to love a woman—give your heart to her, your writing suffers. I've never known why but it is why *Strangers Combined* didn't go anywhere and why *Because of Her* isn't going anywhere."

My jaw clenches. "What am I supposed to do with this information?"

Matt picks up his silverware. I knew this lunch was going to affect my career but I didn't know to this degree.

"I'm letting you in on what I've picked up on. It's up to you to make a decision," he says.

"I'm not letting go of Ava," I snap. Even though I damn well should as liking Ava so much is affecting my career.

Loving Ava so much is affecting your career, my subconscious rebels.

I work my jaw, unable to look Matt eye to eye. "Am I fired or not?"

"You're on a close watch, Cole. What you gave me in the beginning had the most potential I've ever seen from you. I want you to finish *Because of Her* with as much vigor and assurance as when you started. I'm not suggesting you break up and start over with someone else to write better. I'm suggesting you may be moving too fast. And it *may be* best to slow things down."

Matt has no clue how slow me and Ava are going. If I can't kiss her, I can't love her.

All I know about Ava is Henry and her dream of the suburbs. All she knows about me is I'm a writer and my parents are dead. Have I been holding back on her?

I have more to offer, I've had more life experience versus growing up in a foster home. Ava is always interested in my childhood and parents. They died last year. There will never be enough time to grieve and if Ava wants to know, it may be because she wants to help carry my burden.

I knew how important Ava introducing me to Henry was, and I'm grateful for the opportunity to know her better. She doesn't have much to share, growing up in the system doesn't provide vacations and positive memories, while I had a full childhood.

I went to prom and traveled throughout the country while Ava continued re-reading the same books.

"Time to go back to the office," Matt says, tearing me from my reverie with one final thought.

I've begun to fall for Ava Hill—hard.

CHAPTER 15
Cole

I haven't left the inside of my head since leaving lunch with Matt. My career and my woman are fighting for attention in my brain. What I can do? What I will do? What—

"Ow!"

I catch my side where Ava elbowed me. I'm walking her home after seeing a movie—what movie? What actors? Couldn't tell ya.

"Now who's in their head," she smirks.

I think hard on what I heard her say last. "Um...Did you say something about peeing in someone's shoes?"

I open her building door when I hear the beep and follow her up to her apartment. I got building privileges around two weeks ago and we've subconsciously started taking the stairs to prolong our goodbye. She's right, I have been in my head. I guess it's true what people say about couples copying each others habits.

"I said I peed in his shoes."

"You peed in someone's shoes?"

She holds eye contact without blinking then breaks. Playing me again. I wish I wasn't so gullible. Although with Ava, I've learned anything is possible.

"I didn't really, I was trying to get your attention," she says.

"I was listening—"

Ava's sharp eyes silence me.

"Sorry," I say, leaning over to kiss the top of her her head. Without knowing when, I've been able to taste parts of Ava without her flinching away. No more than a taste of her vanilla scent.

"Are you okay, Cole," she asks.

As much fun as Ava and I have had together it has *only* been fun. Neither of us have taken the jump to amend our burdens. If I'm not willing to give up Ava, I might as well give in. For all she knows I don't cook, I'm a writer and I hate breaking the law; which is true. I've never dived into my upbringing with my parents, childhood bullies or the uncertainties of my career.

"I'm not getting anywhere at work," I admit.

Ava's thumb brushes over my knuckles. "I'm sure it will turn around soon. It's only a matter of time."

Until I get fired, I finish mentally. I smile down at Ava because her encouragement and naiveté make me believe things could be so easy—only a matter of time before I complete my first novel without losing my job. Only a matter of time before

I admit my true feelings to the woman attached to me and they're reciprocated.

"What is it you usually write about? Any theme or a particular genre?"

"I don't even know anymore," I relent.

Ava stops me on the third floor and wraps her arms around me. "Stop beating yourself up. Try writing about what you know right now." My heart leaps when she hugs me closer. "Take your time."

I kiss the top of her head again. She doesn't let go of me while we make our way down the hall to her door. I lift her to stand on my shoes and make our way down the hall—her laughing into my chest where we're sealed.

When we stop at her apartment number Ava says, "Thanks for walking me home."

I secure my hold on her a beat longer before she steps off my shoes. "Ava, you don't have to thank me anymore. It's my pleasure." I guide my hand down her cheek and move her braids behind her back, crawling my fingers to the back of her neck where goosebumps follow. Her breath catches and her tongue slides across her supple bottom lip. I bite mine to keep from groaning out loud. "Are you going to bed or can I—"

"Good night, Cole."

Ava slips into her apartment and closes the door on my statement and building libido.

When I get back to my studio, I'm drawn to my laptop and more story spills out of me—the most words I've written in weeks. There are words and emotions pouring out of me through my fingertips.

I stop short when I type 'Ava' instead of Aniya, my protagonist.

Ah fuck.

Because of Her is about Ava.

How the fuck did I let this happen?

Because of Ava I have lost track of my career.

Because of Ava I have emerged from the gray days of mourning.

Shit. Shit. Shit.

Talk about mixing business with pleasure.

Aniya may have grown up in a neglected home, is incredibly beautiful, blocks intimacy, and attracts danger around every corner; she also has hazel eyes. Ava's eyes are a deep dark brown with a hint of yellow around the irises.

And I wouldn't say Ava avoids intimacy, she's more careful. Careful is nice because four months with Rachel we'd already said 'I love you' and she was decorating my apartment to the point I didn't recognize my own home. Which in hindsight, should have been a red flag. I wanted to see my home versus what our place could look like together. That's not the building blocks for something to last.

Ava doesn't need to be saved. Or...doesn't need me to save her. I have a feeling Ava has me right where she wants me.

CHAPTER 16
Ava

"Cole seriously, at this point I will pay for White Castle. I am so freaking hungr—"

"We're here," he says.

I walk through the door he's holding open. Uhm...The Falcon, really? I know he spends a lot of time here. Which then shifts my thoughts straight to alcoholism. I shake my head and follow behind, remembering he said he needed to run *home* and get his wallet.

"You live in a bar," I say.

"I live above a bar. Come on. It'll be quick." He takes my hand and walks me through the bar—slapping backs and shaking hands with various consumers. In the back corner there's a chipped door painted hunter green. Cole removes his keys from his pocket to unlock it. Up fifteen steps are three doors—apartment 1, 2, and 3. Huh, shut me up.

Cole unlocks the middle door, rushes inside to close his laptop on the table in front of the couch. I haven't heard or sensed anymore of his inner turmoil regarding his story. I half expect he's gotten past his writers block and will let me take a gander soon.

Looking around, I hug myself. I've lived in some small places and even I feel claustrophobic in his studio. There's too much furniture and not enough light due to the exposed brick walls and no window. Plus, with Cole throwing around clothes and loose papers to find his wallet, I feel like I'm on the verge of being buried alive.

Instead, I think about 'the best tacos in Indy' he promised me for tonight's dinner reservation.

I never gave much thought to what Cole's apartment would look like. Just well kept. I. Was. Wrong. Clothes thrown about, dishes overflowing in the sink and a full ashtray that if Cole knocks over in his haste I will vomit. I'm not taken aback he smokes cigarettes, Casey always has a pack on hand; damaging his breath, lungs, my duvet.

I'm not shocked nor impressed, I'm only hungry and I'd like to leave right now—

Really. I release a steadying breath through my nose. Cole's wallet is atop the entry table. I roll my eyes.

"Uh, Cole." He turns to me with his wallet in my hand. Cole releases a breath and takes his wallet from me.

His lips find my cheek and if I wasn't leaning against the door frame, I would have crumbled from jelly legs. God, he has the softest lips. "Thank you, are you ready?"

My stomach grumbles in answer. "Nice place," I say with a wink.

"Oh uh—" he waves around the disarray of his abode. I capture his hand and lead us down the stairs.

I take a heaping bite of my third hongos taco as its been an hour and a half since we were supposed to be at our reservation. When we got back to the street outside The Falcon, our Uber kept circling the block without stopping. I dressed in a midi teal dress with nude block heels I don't have much experience in, so I didn't want to walk anymore. Once getting a ride and arriving at the restaurant, Cole slammed the car door on my dress resulting in a slit up my right leg.

All the hassle evaporated once I took my first bite. I close my eyes and savor the abundance of flavor and spice—pickled jalapeño, epazote, queso, wafting throughout my mouth. Then it's gone. I need more.

"Good," Cole asks.

I nod, trying to chew and swallow before speaking. "Oh my god, Cole. So good."

"The best tacos in Indy?"

"In the world. For all I know."

Cole reaches over with his napkin to dab my chin. He pulls back with taco sauce damped on the cloth. I cower further into my meal until Cole's finger at my chin guides me to his consoling wink. We keep eating our meals and when Cole rakes my hand across the table, I don't remember I should be keeping him at arms length.

Chapter 17
Cole

Ava is still wiping her chin and cheeks well after dinner. As I'm walking her home, she's checking herself in every passing reflection. I didn't mean to make her self-conscious. I was impressed.

Ava had a plate full of carbs, and the first bite made me disappear for all intense and purposes. She cleaned her plate and then made a joke about getting three more tacos to freeze at home. I howled with laughter while our waiter looked between us dubious.

"What are you smiling at," Ava asks.

I shake my head from the memory.

"Any project updates?"

I smile down to the muse Ava doesn't know she is. She wipes her face again and I take her hand to kiss her palm.

"I'll be published in no time," I say.

Ava jumps and wraps her arms around my neck, pulling me down into her chest. She's proud of me.

"I'm so proud of you." She steps back, I take her hand to keep contact. "Is there a chance I could take a peek or is only Matt—ow Cole! Geez."

The thought of Ava reading my story led my reflexes to crush her fingers in my hand. She snatches out of my grasp and flex her digits in and out, while I reign myself in. What if she saw herself in *Because of Her* and thought I was using her? She'd leave me. She wouldn't trust me. She can't know yet.

"Sorry—I'm sorry Ava." I reach for her and she hides her hand in her chest. I put my hands on her shoulders and slowly make my way down until her hand is back in mine. "Uhm, not yet."

"Okay...no big deal. No need to Hulk out," she says with a smile and I relax.

I've walked Ava home and up 53 steps 67 times already. She slams her door on me faster than I can say good night. And I go home without a backward glance so I don't turn around and beg for her touch. Tonight, more than ever I don't want our date to end. If I could only convince her that if she were to give herself to me, I'd be sure to take care of her. Be her anchor in this sea of life.

My shoulder lands on her door frame and I wait for the inevitable. "Good night, Ava."

"Uhm...not yet." My words tossed back at me brings me up short.

Ava closes our gap, her chest presses against mine and I freeze, not wanting to do anything to change her mind for whatever is coming. Her arms come around my neck, and when our foreheads come together, I cannot breathe. Then, oh so gently her velvet lips meet mine. Our moment is brief. When she starts to pull away, I don't let her go.

My mouth claims hers. With a sudden gasp, my tongue takes the invite to attach to hers. Crossing this line has me hungry for more. I steel her against the wall, her leg wraps around mine and her slow grind against my zipper is almost too much to bear. To control myself, and the situation, I find the strength to push her away, taking a step back. We've gone from zero to 100, and I abhor to think I've overstepped her boundaries or—

Ava's finger is at my chin. Gradually, I bring my eyes to hers and notice she's smiling.

"I'm sorry," I say, sheepishly.

Her hand cups my cheek. She still hasn't caught her breath. "Don't be."

"I've uh...really wanted to kiss you," I admit.

"I wasn't ready." I nod. Because she kissed me once doesn't mean she'd kiss me again. I need to learn to keep myself under— "I'm ready now."

That's all the permission I need.

CHAPTER 18
Ava

"We kissed!"

OH MY GOD! I haven't stopped smiling since Cole kissed me two days ago. Two days ago, Cole Tace Roberts claimed my mouth as his. What else is there to think about?

I can't talk to Casey about Cole's gentle yet urgent lips, nor the growl hidden beneath a moan making me weak. Henry got the full account as he was laying in my bed when I got inside. He's got a good ear but I needed more than what my canine could offer.

Which is why I'm here in front of Blaine. Except I'm not looking for him to be an unpaid therapist. I don't have anything to rehash or relearn trauma responses. I need to do the one thing I've never had the chance to do: gossip. Casey wouldn't let me gush incessantly; assuming the likelihood wouldn't last long.

"Ava, you sound happy and I'm happy for you. Is everything else okay," Blaine asks.

"Everything else like what? Cole and I kissed for like four minutes!"

Blaine shifts in his chair. He has three daughters. It's highly unlikely I'm the first to talk his ear off about a guy. He clocks the time and offers me the floor with the sway of his hand.

"Tell me all about it," he says.

46 minute gossip sesh commenced.

Time flies when you're in a delusional mindset with your faux boyfriend. One of the top things I enjoy about Cole is how he gives me something new to experience.

Per Cole's silent promise, we drove three hours north for me to experience the Indiana Dunes for the first time. I'm not used to being in a car for long periods as I'm walking distance to the places I frequent. To rid myself of the confinement sitting in his Nissan Altima, I read my latest library book until I fell asleep. When we head back, I promised myself to stay awake throughout the drive to see more of the state I've always lived in without seeing much of what it has to offer.

While Cole spent the morning out getting supplies for our beach picnic, I went out to buy my first swimsuit. Growing up I'd wear a large T-shirt and shorts to run through the water hose. At the store, I was immediately doused by different colors, patterns, and straps. Why so many straps? I only have two shoulders.

Within two hours, and getting stuck in two different suits, I decided on a navy two piece. Scoop neck top and brief bottoms. To stay close to my roots, I still paired them with an oversized T-shirt.

"You okay?"

Since getting out of the car I've been speechless at the vision of vast open water, and a peek of Chicago. The weather is a bit balmy, but combined with the sea breeze makes it bearable. We're in the middle of May so there aren't too many families around. And the view, it's breathtaking. If I could swim, I'd start pulling my arms against the currents and never look back.

"Ava?"

I turn around to Cole on the sand prepping our blanket and the food he packed for our beach day.

I sit and watch him remove two bottles of water, sunscreen and peanut butter and jelly sandwiches from the basket he packed.

"This is beautiful. A piece of heaven on earth." My smile isn't forced or fake, like most of my time with Cole, it's content...for the moment. "Do we just sit here or..."

"Now." Cole stands and pulls his shirt from over his head. For the most part, I go out of my way to stay hydrated, having a water jug in my bag and on my desk at work. My eyes pop at Cole shirtless. I'm fighting to stay still when I really need to plunge myself into the sea to cool off. His arms, thin yet muscular; plus a solid chest, and a full six pack has me flushed.

Cole snaps his fingers in my face as he joins me on the blanket. "Eyes up here," he says, pointing to his eyes.

I wipe the corner of my mouth. "Boy boo."

He tugs the hem of my shirt. "Your turn."

We lock eyes and I raise my arms above my head. Cole takes his time coming closer to me and pulls my shirt up from the hem. His fingertips leave goosebumps along my sides and a craving in my groin. I yank my arms out of my sleeves and head out of my collar to keep me from going X-rated on a family beach. I fling my braids out of my face and secure them in a high ponytail.

"Have you put on sunscreen," Cole asks, folding my shirt and placing it on top of his.

"No." I've never worn sunscreen. I've never touched sand. And I've only pictured views this vibrant from the books I've read.

Cole shakes the bottle of sunscreen, smacking the bottom with his palm. In no way, shape, or form do I surmise his hand doing the same to a specific body part of mine. When he pops open the cap, I snatch it from him.

"I'll do it," I say.

He leans back on his hands and watches me pour a large amount of cream into my hand. I begin rubbing my arms, belly, and shoulders. I stroke and stroke and rub the lotion to no avail. I look up to Cole for help. I look like I've been doused with a bag of flour.

"Less is more," Cole says through a laugh. His fingers start at my shoulder, massaging down my arm, taking the excess with him to distribute on his own. He repeats with my other. Then rubs my shoulders, moving the sunscreen down my back. The warmth from the sun is the least of my worries now. My eyes blink open from their reverie when his hands are no longer gliding along my body. Cole turns around and I press my hands into his back to transfer the excess cream from my hands onto him.

"Wanna try the water," Cole asks, when we're both lathered up.

My previous excitement of swimming endlessly settles into reality. *I can't swim.* "It's probably cold," I deflect.

"You'll never know until you find out." His face transforms from tempest to mischief. I'm too late to dissect further because Cole has me over his shoulder in one swift movement.

Being skin to skin, my body freezes instead of continuing its heated thought process when he was putting lotion on me. I haven't been this close to someone since...Mitchell. Cole and I have only toed the line of intimacy. Whatever comfortability we've built crumbles at the realization that Mitchell was the last man to touch me, have me, and the horrible ending I woke up to. The ending always following my best of intentions.

"No! No Cole." I'm wailing and kicking, not caring who hears or sees. I want him to let me go. "Let me go! Put me down. Now!" I open my mouth to scream when he's already stopped walking.

"Shh. Shh." Cole slides me down his bare chest. I run around him, back to our blanket and cover myself with a towel. I keep my forehead to my knees to avoid the lingering stares I feel from my outburst.

"Shit, Ava I'm sorry." I sense Cole without looking up to see he's there. He hesitantly rubs my back, starting with a couple fingers then his entire hand to help soothe me. "I was kidding, Ava. I wouldn't do anything without making sure it's okay with you first."

"I know Cole."

"Will you look at me?" I lay my temple on my knees to face his direction. He shields my eyes from the sun so I'll be able to see him better. "I'm sorry."

"I know."

"Will you tell me what happened," he asks. "Was it the water or—"

"I don't like being grabbed unaware."

"Oh...Did that happen a lot in the group home?"

I scoff. "It happens a lot being a woman."

Cole lowers his head. "Right. I'm sorry."

Although, we may have discussed ghosts and free health care, we have not ventured to exes. And I don't want this to be the moment we start.

I'm certain I've ruined the day. Cole places a saran wrapped PB&J near my feet; and slowly I unravel myself. "Thank you."

He takes a big bite of his sandwich, I move closer and lay my head on his shoulder. We both release a huge breath.

CHAPTER 19
Cole

When Nugget gets back from the bathroom he claps me on the back before regaining his spot by Gail. "It's time, brother!"

I jump. "Bro, did you wash your hands?" I've seen too much from my lifelong friend, helps to be sure.

"Funny," he says. "You're stalling."

"Stalling what?"

Nugget and Gail look at me without blinking. Nugget's eyes go glassy and I'm not sure if it's from our staring contest or emotions he's trying to mask. Then again he called me 'brother.' Which means his drunkenness could turn soapy, or he's another Stella away from slobbering in Gail's ear to go home with him. If he were to succeed he'll salute me with a 'farewell brother.'

"We want to meet Ava," Gail says.

"Ahh." The mention of Ava's name takes me back to our time at the beach. Spending time with Ava is never boring and each beautiful minute is easily halted by something she's avoiding to tell me. Thankfully, by the end of our beach day we were back to being an infatuated couple. Her shrieks of horror when our bodies touched was the complete opposite of what I felt having her soft skin against mine. My body's reaction was lit with lust having her behind against my face and her thick thighs trapped under my arm. I wonder if there's a chance we'll ever get past her past.

"And I miss you man," Nugget hiccups.

I laugh around another sip of Stella. Its been a long week for Nugget, Gail and myself. When I sent them a text for happy hour they replied with a five minute ETA. Happy hours three dollar pints turned to ten dollar pitchers and now it's 1am. Nugget has the hiccups and Gail is ready to pretend she's the latest late night talk show host. And I have unfortunately left Ava seven voicemails plus three text messages. Sarah must like to see us suffer because why hasn't she cut us off?

"It's the only way we'll get to see you more. Instead of splitting your time with us and Ava, we could all get the chance to hangout—"

"Until you dump her," Nugget says.

Gail smacks him upside the head. "He's not dumping Ava."

"I'm not dumping Ava," I agree.

"Cole dumped you and you've been on my couch bingeing *Scandal* with me."

Why am I always drinking when Gail confesses something about Nugget I'm not prepared for. However, this time I spit out on my friends rather than myself.

"You've been watching *Scandal*," I cackle.

"No," Nugget says, glaring at Gail for blabbing.

"Uh huh. So, tell me Braxton. Are you Team Fitz or Team Jake?"

"How do *you* know about Fitz and Jake," he challenges.

I stop and swallow hard. "I am a writer and Shonda Rhimes is a visionary. What's your excuse?"

Also, I subconsciously admit, what man doesn't get a tad invested in the shows his significant other is watching? Nuggets cheeks are growing to match the shade of his hair at my off the cuff comeback.

"The point is," Gail continues, bringing us back. "He misses his bro, Cole. And I miss you, too."

They both ambush me with their puppy dog eyes and I fold like I'm made of origami. When Nugget and Gail began dating he couldn't wait to introduce me to her. He didn't leave me hanging to fend for myself. And now I have two of the best people in my life. With Ava included, we could be the Fantastic Four.

"The three of us will hang out tomorrow—"

"Yay," Nugget claps.

"And," Gail prods.

"And you can meet Ava," I say.

"Really," they respond.

Nugget pushes Gail away. "Not you."

Gail shoves him back. "Shut up."

Even when they'd date, Nugget and Gail would rarely fight together; but they will fight over me.

"I love you guys," I say.

"Hey y'all, tequila," Sarah says with a tray of shots.

"Yes," Nugget delights.

"No," Gail and I say.

"Come on. We're here already," Nugget says.

"We've been here all day," I say.

Nugget holds up one finger promising one and done. I roll my eyes and touch my finger to his like ET.

"Shit," Gail says, chugging her glass of water.

The quality time Nugget, Gail and I will be sharing tomorrow will be spent nursing tonights hangover.

CHAPTER 20
Ava

I set my phone face down on the coffee table.

"No answer," I say. I'm not ready to look up to Casey. I know he'll be upset. And I know it's my fault. I should have stuck to his plan. Cole and I kiss once—one time for four minutes and I've used it as the only fuel to prove he likes me, trusts me. Cole's texts and voicemails from last night were incoherent. Were they sent on purpose? On accident? Meant for someone else who's able to assimilate his ramblings?

I wish I hadn't reacted the way I did at the beach. Cole shouldn't have seen that side of me—a part of me. Slowly but surely he's working his way through the facade Casey has ingrained in me.

"How many times have you called," Casey asks.

"Five," I lie, and Casey knows. I can feel his eyeballs searing a hole in my brain. "Eleven."

"God Ava."

I look up to defend myself. "It's the same amount of times he's called me. What's the problem?"

Casey finds his eyes through his locs to rub out his frustration. The gray clouds through the window mimicking both our mindset. "Ugh, damn it."

I'm not only anxious of Casey's reaction, but Cole's absence as well.

"Tell me what you did? What happened," Casey asks.

I take a beat to myself before getting the subject of the matter over with—his disappointment in me. And I tell him the truth. "Nothing outside of what you told me to do. We're taking it slow and you know...I mean, we've only kissed once—one night. We kissed one night for like four minutes."

My cheeks flush at the memory. No matter how I feel about Cole right now, the amount of care and consideration he caressed me with last week still gets me hot and—

"That was always your problem, Ava," Casey's backlash chills me. "You have to learn to wait. If you can't wait, neither will he and you'll be right back where you were headed when Mitchell left. Which cannot happen this time."

"It won't," I seethe. Casey knows not to bring up an ex once they're gone. And due to the Mitchell reminder at the beach, I'm more sensitive than usual.

As much fun and time I've spent with Cole I know it's not for real. It can't be. No matter how carried away I get, Cole and I will not end up together. The only thing he's given me to take is trust. Trust there is someone walking among this earth without a bad habit I feel the need to break. And who will give me the attention and care the way Cole has—excluding the last fourteen hours.

"Just wait, Ava! I have a feeling Cole isn't going anywhere and if he does I know you'll be able to get him back," Casey says.

Even under his scrutiny, Casey still believes in me. "How do you have so much faith in me?"

Casey closes in and takes one of my hands I have clenched in my lap. "I have faith in you because I know you won't let me down. You wouldn't be able to forgive yourself. And I won't be able to survive this time."

The only other person Casey has survived is Rayvin.

"Have you been thinking about her?"

In response, Casey's fingers crush mine in his. What is with these Roberts men always going for the metacarpals. I flinch, not pulling away.

"No, I haven't." He throws my hand away and stands. "I have to go."

Casey slams the door on his way out and I'm back to staring at my ringless phone.

CHAPTER 21
Casey

"We. Hate. Rayvin!"

I'm out of breath pacing back and forth in front of Blaine.

Why is it so hard for people to listen? I asked Ava to never bring up Rayvin and she thinks because she didn't say her name I won't be affected. Rayvin has always affected me. She used me like she did the others. I was never special. I was another person on her rotation.

"Casey, *you* hate Rayvin," Blaine deadpans.

I pause to the right of him. "Aren't you supposed to be on my side?"

I'm a mess. Some patients need years to figure out what plummeted them into their black hole. All it took for me was the second Rayvin broke my heart in unmanageable pieces. I became *more* unapproachable and guarded and I can't get my therapist to hate her?!

"I don't take sides," he says.

"Pssh. You're always on Ava's side."

"Ava is happy. Our sessions have gone from healthy boundaries to gushy chitchat. Cole makes her happy and it's all because of you. How does that make you feel?"

"Peachy," I spit.

Blaine nods. "Okay shall we indulge in Rayvin, Ava, or Ava and Cole?"

I fall face first on the couch across from Blaine and scream into the cushion.

CHAPTER 22
Ava

Henry is a playboy. He will bark at his fellow canine as if he could take her out to dinner and a movie, and today at South Street Square he's spotted a freshly puffed poodle he refuses to let be. I picked a tall tree full of shade to read under for lunch and his persistence is ruining my zen.

"Henry—hush." I don't look up from the magazine I've been trying to devour because that's what he wants—me to break. His bark turns into a whine. He's acting hopeless now. Like mother, like son. I shake off the insecurity of another day passing without hearing from Cole before it takes hold. "Henry, please don't do this to me. It's not like y'all can make a family, you're fixed big guy. I don't even know her owner, they could be...vegan." Henry drones some more. "Plus she is way out of your league—"

"Ava!"

I freeze and barely raise my eyes above my magazine to see Cole Roberts waving and heading our way. The sun hits him at the right spot to highlight his body, making him look like an angel descending from above. He sidles next to me, wraps his arm around my shoulders and pulls me in for a kiss on the lips. My muscles are frozen. Henry's wail seizes and he goes to lay on Cole's feet. *Cole's feet?*

I haven't heard or thought of—thought much of Cole since I called him one final time when Casey left and it went straight to voicemail. In the last three days, I've read five books and spent some one on one time with Henry. He's gotten the prince treatment: his coat is brushed, cut, and he's proud owner of three new chew toys.

And Cole arrives out of thin air to kiss me?

"Uh, Cole?"

He kisses me again, lingering against my lips with a smile before pulling away.

"Hi—" Cole sees the magazine in my hand. "Ava, you...you're reading my magazine?"

I hardly spoil myself with luxuries and never because of someone else; the curiosity got the better of me. I subscribed to his magazine to read the stories already in print, since he's keeping whatever he's currently writing close to his chest—and for his boss.

I subscribe to his life's work and he doesn't contact me for three days. I'm torn between the argument I'm having with myself, Cole's beautiful grin, and the lingering sensation from his lips on mine. I'm out numbered.

"Wow...you're amazing. And thank you," he says.

"How did you find me," I ask sharply.

"Greg let me know."

Greg. I release a degree of animosity through my nose. The relief I was enduring under Cole's gaze and kisses halt at the mention of Greg's name. I can't help but work with him except he spends his free time threatening to give Henry away to someone else. His favorite joke no one ever laughs at. Especially when it went so far, I was in the fetal position crying thinking Henry was gone forever when he was actually at the groomers. I can't stand Greg.

"Total breach of privacy," I say.

Cole tucks me closer under his arm and unbeknownst to me, my body relaxes.

"Desperate times," he says. *As if I'm one to talk.* "You miss me?"

I scoff and remove myself from his embrace. So he knows he's ghosted me the last three days. "Yea, you sure know how to make a girl wait. Don't you?"

"Ahh. You're my girl, come here." He brings me back to where I escaped.

You're my girl. Cole gave us a label. I'm his girl. My body heats and tingles.

"I'm sorry about the weekend. Nugget got us carried away."

I lay my head on his shoulder. "I was worried about you."

He kisses the top of my head, tucking us into the trunk of the tree. "You don't have to worry about me. I'm not one to ghost out of nowhere."

"You'll give me a two weeks notice or something," I say.

Cole laughs. "You don't have to worry about anything of the sort."

Because I'm his girl. I lift my head and his lips come down on mine. I situate myself to his side and across the park, the shadow I know is Casey, is looking at us. I stiffen a bit, unable to read his expression from so far away. But the majority of my body is relieved because Cole is back.

CHAPTER 23
Cole

I figured after my drunken voicemails and missing Ava's calls, it'd be a better act of service to show up for Ava rather than the potential of a miscommunicated text. She started put out when I showed up at the park. Firm lips, leaning away from me, eyes squinting. Then I think she found me tracking her down to be romantic.

"You know guys, I'm pretty sure we're the only people ever at this booth. I don't think I've ever seen anyone else here since I've started living upst—"

"Yea yea, were the diverse version of *How I Met Your Mother*. Anyway!" Nugget interjects. I was rambling to avoid Nugget and Gail's scrutiny, except I knew better. Although, my statement is valid. We keep the same booth, even though they've opened the patio. The air conditioning and not being beaten down by the sun helps us pace ourselves. Unlike the college kids needing the railing to hold themselves up. They'll learn in their own time. "Ava didn't complain at all? No tears or breaking your mother's china?"

Nugget is convinced Ava is hiding something. Whatever I tell them is combated with something so far out of the ordinary to make sense. Breaking my mothers china? Serial dater? Ava is not the villain of my story.

"My mothers china? Bro, I don't even have access to my mother's china! And what do you take her for?"

"Hell, she called you twenty times last weekend."

"It was ten times and I called her eleven. I should have checked in way before today. It made complete sense for her to have been worried," I say.

"Pssh. You think she's perfect, so you don't see the signs," he says.

"She is..."

She is. For the most part. Nugget rolls his eyes and takes his Stella to the head. I take a half second to myself to think about the one thing Ava and I haven't done with all the time we've spent together.

"Hey. I saw that," Gail says.

Shit, caught. A half second too long apparently. "Saw what?"

"There was a look—spill! How many other people is she dating?"

"Why does serial dating have to be Ava's thing?"

Nugget pokes Gail in the ribs with his elbow. "I said the same thing." They give each other a cocky high five. If only they used their gifts for good.

"Ava is not dating anyone else—unless you count Henry," I say.

Gail's elbow nudges Nugget's ribs. "I told you." Their palms slap twice.

"He's a St. Bernard."

Both of their faces fall at the same time.

"Uh huh. Nice try. Like I said, Ava is perfect—perfect for me..." And as much as I care for her I am still a man. And since I saw her body in a bikini I've been itching for the chance to explore. "It's nothing major. It's not like she's a superficial—"

"Ugh, remember Tiffany," Gail says. "'Oh, I'm so pretty. Oh, The North Pole isn't real.' Ugh, shut the fu—"

"Okay. And she's not compulsive—"

Nugget cuts me off this time. "Ugh, Rachel, she—"

"Stop. Ava isn't anything either of you could come up with. You've tried and failed multiple times."

"Then tell us," Gail says.

"Ava is—yea, I mean she's a little crazy—" I forge on when Nugget opens his mouth. "In a fun way." He closes his mouth and wiggles his eyebrows. *I wish.* "She's...guarded? I think that's the proper word for it."

"Guarded," Nugget sounds out the word.

"Oh, you're good," Gail says.

"Really?"

"Actually, in my unpopular opinion—"

Gail jams two pretzel bites in Nugget's mouth before he can offer his opinion to contribute to my anxiety.

"Absolutely not. Ava is guarded. So what? What if she had webbed feet."

Nugget and I gag in unison, "Ugh!"

"Exactly. You have to learn how and when to fight your battles," she says.

Gail's logic makes sense. And if there's one thing Nugget's done right is bringing her in. I shudder at the years of Nugget's advice about women and where its gotten me. He's had me slapped, kneed in my privates and running away from three separate houses on three separate occasions bare assed. With Gail's coaching, I'll be able to keep Ava around for a long time.

"I really like Ava. Things are going slow..." I clear my throat and lean in—the three of us meeting in the middle of the table, "Physically."

Nugget swallows. "Yikes."

"Shut up. It's not a huge deal because..." *I love her*—whoa!...Where did that come from? "I'm hanging in there. Literally."

Nugget reaches for my hand across the table. "If you want my advice—"

"No," Gail and I yell.

Nugget looks to Gail accusingly and she winks.

"I mean, no thank you Nugg. I'm okay and Ava is okay. I shouldn't even be complaining, she's amazing."

"Okay, if you *were* looking for advice—I would say do something to leave her wanting to get you past her front door," he suggests.

"Like what?"

Nugget shrugs. "I can't do all the work." He hops out of out booth and waves us over to an empty pool table. "Let's play a game."

I agree and before I leave the table, Gail places her hand over mine. I stop and I look towards my light at the end of the tunnel.

"Or you can wait for Ava to come to you. We all know it's only a matter of time before she will. You got this."

CHAPTER 24

Ava

"Did you have fun tonight," Cole asks.

"I always do when I'm with you," I say, fighting a yawn.

We decided to Uber back to my house instead of walking because I'm on the verge of a food coma and I'd rather fall asleep in my bed than on the street.

My phone dings twice, alerting me to a message. Pulling it out from my jacket pocket, I see Casey's name on the screen, and slide to the other side of the cab to read his text.

> **Casey**
> enjoy the rest of your night, thank you
> for all you're doing

I set my phone in my lap face down, give Cole a weak smile and stare out the side window watching the city pass by for the rest of the drive.

When we pull up outside my building, Cole gets out first to round the car and open my door. With my hand in his, I become unsettled by the thought of being left tonight. Any other evening, I'd come home and wait for Casey to debrief.

There's nothing and no one waiting for me. If Casey had texted me earlier, I'd have brought Henry home for the weekend. Tonight, it's only me.

A night to enjoy myself. Although, that'd only truly happen if Casey told me this was all over. Whether either of us like it or not, I'm dating his brother, regardless of the pretenses.

I can't figure what else there is to know. I know I don't want to tell Cole good night without him knowing I care about him, before everything blows up in my face.

"Good night Ava," Cole says. His lips find my cheek and I savor his heat.

"Do you want to come upstairs?"

"I always walk you to your door," he says.

I bite my lip to keep from laughing at his innocence. Of course me inviting him upstairs doesn't register I'm inviting him inside my apartment. It took well over three months for me to kiss him.

How has he stuck around this long? What does he want from me? What does he see in me to walk me to my door, check in on Henry or text me good night right before I lay my head on my pillow? He does so much for a short-term commitment.

"I mean come upstairs to my apartment—inside my apartment," I clarify.

Cole's smile stretches wide. My, oh my, this man has a beautiful set of teeth: straight, clean, bright.

"Ava, are you inviting me past that door?" He's pointing to my building.

"You've made it past that door before."

He runs to our Uber, I'm assuming to let him know we doesn't have to wait; then runs back to take my hand and rushes us inside and up three flights to my apartment.

"This door?" He points with his thumb.

I hold back a laugh. "Only if you want to."

I take his hands on my cheeks and open lips inviting my tongue to meet his as a yes. He kisses me on the nose, then says, "Its been a long time coming."

I push him away involuntarily, seeping back to my last night with Mitchell.

"I want you to spend the night with me, Mitchell," I said.

His smile undid me. It shot through my heart and cracked me open. Those three words threatening to jump off the tip of my tongue.

"Its been a long time coming Ava," he said.

I waited for the words to let me know I'm as important to him as he is to me.

"I love you," he said.

Before I fell asleep in his arms and after I gave him my heart, he claimed my body.

"Ava, are you okay," Cole asks.

Cole's face is honest and his eyes are curious, as I bring myself back to the present. His hand rests on the small of my back to make sure if I fall, he'll catch me.

I remember looking into Mitchell's 'honest' eyes, if I had looked a little deeper I would have seen the person he truly is.

Cole's concern doesn't drop, his thumb sweeping across my cheek. I force myself to believe Cole is different and I'm not using him because we're both keeping things from each other.

"I'm fine," I say, and unlock my apartment. "Come in."

CHAPTER 25
Cole

Here's what I've cherished about Ava before stepping into her apartment: her tenacity to complete her goals, the fact she even has goals, and her appetite for literature.

And to see her bookshelf littered with timeless romance novels—*Pride and Prejudice, Everything Everything, The Notebook*—it's evident Ava is hoping for her own story as ever-lasting, without it having come to fruition. I can't imagine the sort of rejection she's endured considering how beautiful and engaging she is. I'm always waiting for the next chance to be with her again.

Ava's essence is all over her apartment: framed photos of her and Henry; a disintegrated baby blanket over the arm of the couch; and vanilla in the air. Ava herself is also all over her apartment; from her bedroom to change to the kitchen where I hear glasses clinking together.

"You read a lot of books, and watch a lot of movie adaptions of the books," I say, noticing the DVD's accompanying their book titles.

"The only movies I've seen are based on the books I've read." I hear from the kitchen. "Plus Tom Cruise and the classic repeats on Bounce. And Lifetime, as you well know."

"And I happen to see a specific pattern," I mutter to myself. "Lover of love stories."

I turn around to Ava when I hear glasses being sat down. She's on her couch in a T-shirt so large it falls to the middle of her thighs. I have to fight to keep my eyes above her neck. The only light left on is the lamp by the couch, setting a sensual tone.

"You know I have a favorite romance movie myself," I say.

"You'd admit you have one," she asks, while grabbing her braids to fasten in a low ponytail.

"Guess," I say, taking the other glass of wine as I sit.

"A classic," she starts.

"Mhmm." I tilt my glass toward her and we clink. "Guess."

Post sip she assumes, *Love and Basketball*."

"No," I say, shaking my head.

"*Brown Sugar*."

The side to side of my head doesn't stop. "Imma give you one last chance," I say.

I pause. "*The Wood*," she says.

"You consider *The Wood* a romance movie?"

"Don't you?"

"No. Time's up. It's *Deliver Us From Eva*."

"Ohhhhh...okay then." She laughs into her glass and then we lock eyes.

"B-b-b-bitch. Bitch," we mimic from the movie and fall into each other in hilarity.

"I'm dying. Did you grow up thinking you were as smooth as LL Cool J," she says, moving her ponytail of braids from the nape of her neck to the top of her head.

"A smooth con artist? No."

Ava chokes back on her wine. I slap her back until she catches her breath. "You okay?" She gives me a thumbs up. "Plus, I'd admit he had a redeemable arc."

"You think so," she says.

"Don't you?"

She clears her throat and her smile is cautious. "What about a favorite romance novel?"

"I've been hooked on Tia Williams recently. Her prose is...it's captivating and profound, yet simple. I want to have the same kind of impact on my readers."

"Oh yea I know all about Ms. Williams."

"Bit of a romantic are we," I ask.

"Hmm," she says, leaning her head against the back of the couch. "I think I believe in once upon a time more than happily ever after."

"Explain," I say, assuming the same position, except my eyes are on her and she's looking at the ceiling.

"Happily ever after implies a happy ending. And, tah—" She starts laughing with herself. "Not in this lifetime. Which is why we thank Goddess for romance *fiction*!"

I take her hand and rub my thumb over her knuckles. "Alright, say that again without pretending you're not talking about yourself."

Ava's jaw drops and cuts her eyes to mine. She tries to detach us and I don't let her. On the one hand, I might have caught her off guard; and on the other, I've also given her the opportunity to open up to me. I wait out her hesitation. She pours the remainder of her wine down her throat and says—

"In my dating history...love, er—dating hasn't worked for me when there is one thing they want, thousands of books they've never read or most likely never been taught the importance of pursuing and respecting a woman."

For her to say that to me sends my jaw to the ground. I've read a book. I read books all the time. I'm a writer. Books are my profession and I never thought to take notes on how to woo someone because I pride myself in being a gentleman and respectful to all women.

My parents taught me to open doors, pull out chairs, and they never let me think a woman's body is something I'm entitled to have. I hate that women have to question their value due to how they've been treated. I hate Ava questioning her value with me.

"Or hey," she continues, volume rising, refilling her glass again. She salutes her drink and takes three large pulls. "Maybe it's me!"

"What are you...?"

Ava stretches her collar, I think to attempt seduction, though it's fumbled; and sidles against me, pulling her hair free from its rubber band and shaking it to land on her shoulders. "I look like the one thing a man wants and that's all they see. My brown eyes and smooth skin—"

"They're umber," I say.

Her fire simmers. She's stumped. "What?"

"You're eyes are a shade of umber. And the lining of your irises is a sort of dijon."

"Uhmm." She lowers her head, hiding behind her braids. "Um...No one's ever noticed the yellow. I've always liked it. Thought I was unique; except I always get treated the same—"

I can't take this. "Stop it, Ava!"

"What are you—"

I move her braids behind her shoulder, tilt her chin up and wait for her eyes to meet mine. "No, you can't talk—think of yourself like that. I've never saw you as a...a conquest. I wish I would have seen you coming with the cold coffee headed for my white shirt.

"It was when I saw your eyes, I saw determination. Determination which made me want to take you to dinner. And thank

God you said yes because I love being with you Ava. I love—"
Ah fuck. "I love being with you a lot." Nice save.

Holy crap. I am never speaking again. I never knew I had so many words to describe how I feel about Ava and I sure didn't expect telling her damn near wine drunk. Did she hear me? Does she grasp the weight I'm trying to invoke?

She hasn't blinked or shifted and the silence is suffocating me. I put myself out of my misery.

"I'm going to go—I'm sorry—"

Before I get up from the couch to go home and pray I haven't scared her off, she pulls me into her by my shirt and our lips collide.

Ava takes complete control of me with her body. I taste her wine flavored tongue, my hands work under her shirt to touch her immaculate body and through no recollection of my own, we end up tangled in her bed sheets and with each other.

The woman of my dreams. The body of my fantasies. Two dimples at the curve of her back, peaked mocha nipples pressed against my tongue, goosebumps peppering her skin under my fingertips.

Skin to skin, we're finally catching our breaths after losing track of time and losing ourselves in each other. Ava's head is on my chest. We've been pressed together for a while. I wish it was forever.

I gave myself to Ava. I let her tour my entire body and she gave me hers in return. I've never imagined a bond as strong as what Ava brought for the both of us to enjoy.

My fingertips glide along her spine and I'm waiting for her to break the silence. She doesn't, so I start.

"I'm scared by how much I like you," I say. I hate thinking I'm in a one sided relationship. Of course I enjoyed what Ava gave me, what troubles me is how she feels about herself.

I don't have the capacity to make Ava see herself the way I do. She's beautifully independent, captivating, and well read. I've seen people struggle and break without depth and sincerity. Ava has both on top of being appealing. Her depth and authenticity is what's kept me on her doorstep until she was ready. I knew it'd be a simple price to pay. I'd have waited another five months as long as she'd gift me her company.

I joke and jest with Ava and learn about a different life she had to survive compared to the one I was given. I have a better focus on how to see people of different backgrounds.

The hush of the night has found its way between us even though we're as close as two people can possibly be.

Ava breathes in deeply and on the exhale says, "I'm only scared."

I tense and my body jerks Ava to look up.

"Are you scared of me," I ask.

Ava doesn't say anything. She moves forward to kiss me. Before we get caught up again, I pull back a fraction and my eyes beg her to open up to me. She doesn't talk to me. I let her lips meet mine.

CHAPTER 26
Cole

I am split with emotions. A part of me is happy about another special—phenomenal step Ava and I have taken; the other part is frightened of what she hasn't told me.

"Cole, come to my office," Matt says, passing my cubical with a fresh cup of coffee.

I stand and follow him, attempting to shift my thoughts from the perils of my relationship to what could be coming from my boss. Matt closes the door behind me and works his behemoth shape to sit at his desk. No one at Speck is granted space, we're all crammed on top of each other and with Matt's door closed, I feel like his office has shrunk in size and my stomach feels heavy. I finished *Because of Her* and sent it over to Matt earlier this week. To stay ahead of the game, I've been doing my part in editing before it goes to the entire department.

I've been holding on to 'no news is good news' until Matt can't look me in the eye, and then realize I should have been worried.

"Matt?"

"Cole, you've been here a while and I have come to know you not only as an employee but a friend," Matt says. *Oh no.* "And as your friend, I have to let you know how competitive this market is. Even though we have the opportunity to hire new graduates, we're still small. You aren't getting anywhere quick enough for Speck to keep you on payroll. As your boss, we have to let you go."

My stomach falls in my ass. "No, Matt. Please, you can't—"

Matt lifts his hand to pause my pleading.

"This isn't permanent, Cole. I believe in your manuscript, but it's not complete. Your story ended, it's not finished and I can't keep holding your hand to figure it out. Aniya, your protagonist, has something to confess. She can't only be a neglected child who falls in love, she's hiding something. What is it?"

I fall back into my chair. "I don't know," I confess to Matt and myself.

"Once you figure it out is when your story will be complete and when it'll be fit to publish." Matt stands, offering me his hand. "You have my e-mail. Stay in touch."

When Matt told me the women I date—give my heart to, impacted my writing, I didn't think it was possible to love her so soon. Then it came to be I was writing a version of her story without knowing the truth. Her truth. Ava has completely taken over my life and the only thing I have to show is an unfinished manuscript and now unemployment to boot. I need her answers and my job. I'm already calling her on my way out of Matt's office without shaking his hand. I'm packing up the desk I've inhabited for three years, with my phone pressed between my shoulder and ear waiting for Ava to pick up.

"Hello," she says.

My phone slips and slams on my desk. My hands are shaking as I put my laptop in my backpack. When I tuck my phone against my cheek, Ava's calling my name.

"Cole. Hello?"

"I—uh—I want to see you. Can we meet at your apartment in 15 minutes?"

"Okay, I'm here now. Are you okay Cole?"

I press the button for the elevator. "Yea, I'm on my way."

I catch my phone in my hand and disconnect the call. I step onto the elevator ready to demand the answers from Ava I deserve.

CHAPTER 27
Ava

I go to open my front door, to watch and wait for Cole to arrive. Instead of no one or a scurrying neighbor coming down the hallway, Casey enters and closes the door behind him. I'm instantly on edge not knowing how close Cole could be.

"Casey, you have to go now. Cole will be here any minute," I say.

"I know. I wanted to stop by before he got here."

Wait what. Cole and I just got off the phone. "You know? How do you—Casey, I know you said you'd be around but I hardly ever *see* you. It doesn't make me feel safe."

He rolls his eyes at my statement, not taking me seriously. "Ava, calm down. I'm the safest person you've ever had in your life. Don't talk down to me again."

"That's not how I meant..." I don't have time to get into this right now. "Never mind, I'm sorr—"

"Don't apologize," Casey yells. I jump at his tone. He takes his time to breathe in and out—reigning himself in. "I actually came by to thank you for how well you're doing. We're almost there."

"Almost where?" *What happens next?*

"To tell Cole—"

To tell Cole the truth? Finally! "Are you sure?" I am ecstatic. This will all be over soon.

"Of course I am."

I bite my lip to keep from smiling. Is there a way Cole could forgive me for all I've done to convince him to fall for me? In reality, I'm no better than Mitchell except I feel awful. I want mercy and then a real chance.

"What's that look—what did you do," Casey asks.

I release my lip. "I haven't done anything." Wiping away my glee, I remember. "Uh actually...There was something...uhm..."

"Spit it out!"

"He said..." Casey runs his finger in a circle to urge me forward. "Cole said something and it brought me up short last week." I wave away the thought. "I could be overthinking things."

"Can you tell me what he said, Ava," Casey snaps.

"Chill. He only said..." I clear my throat. "Cole said, 'its been a long time coming.'" I physically use air quotes to highlight Mitchell's words because I'd never say anything to trick someone into sex and leave in the middle of the night. I do not want to be associated with the language of douchebag. Casey is waiting for me to continue. He doesn't note my distress. "It is exactly what Mitchell said the night we—before he left. It could be a universal line."

He exhales, reaches into his back pocket for his box of cigarettes and places one in between his lips. "Ava, you've heard a number of universal lines which should have prompted you not to fall for guys who'd break your heart. And you did, every time."

I bristle internally. I hate when Casey throws my stupidity in my face.

"You're right," I force out.

Casey rolls his eyes as if he's tired of me being upset from what he says. He falls and extends his arms across the couch, blowing a line of smoke from the corner of his mouth.

"Don't sound so broken up, Ava. This is better than anything you've been through previous because you are acting. It's not real. It's revenge," he says, his features transitioning from being annoyed with me to fury; causing a deep chill to come over me. Revenge? I'm not quite sure how me building information and revenge correlate.

"Your master plan is revenge? Revenge on Cole? What does that mean? He hasn't done anything."

"God, shut up Ava."

"Casey! Don't talk to me like—"

"No." He comes to stand over me and I lean back from his advance. "Remember this: Cole is a simple man. And remind me how much luck you've had with men in your life? I am the only one who has ever taken care of you. And don't forget: Cole stole my life—my family! Or did you come down with amnesia after a couple fucks?"

Damn. He's not wrong, but isn't there a way he can explain himself without making me feel worse? Tears threaten to spill down my cheeks. I don't trust my voice to produce coherent words. I look away, crest fallen.

He deflates. "Damnit. I'm sorry Ava."

Casey falls back into the couch, eyes to the ceiling. I wait him out as he takes short drags and long breaths. He shifts on the couch to remove his carton from his back pocket for my center table to catch.

"I'm sorry. It's...ugh, everything about him pisses me the fuck off. I'm always going around and around thinking about why our parents didn't keep me."

His shallow breaths pull me to him and I rub soft circles into his leg with my fingers while tears leak from the corner of his eyes. I begin crying too. I know his pain as an orphan, except for all I know my birth mom died from a persistent customer unwilling to comprehend the word 'no.' She didn't separate me from siblings for an unfathomable reason.

Dating Cole and being a friend to Casey is splitting me in two. Casey needs me to be his person to help. I promised him from the beginning and I intend to keep my word. The fantasy of Cole and I is extinguished.

I remove Casey's tears with my thumb. Slowly, his head turns, our eyes locking. His misguided suffering and restlessness makes me melt. I've always loved Casey for being there for me. We've only been friends, and occasionally I'd wonder why.

Why does he continue to watch me date the wrong guy? Why won't he realize Rayvin was a chapter not the whole story? These questions push me to lean over the final line we've never crossed when he pulls away.

I drop my head. "You've never thought about it?"

Casey stands. Before the depression of rejection settles over my psyche, the side of Casey's mouth ticks. It'd be ambiguous to anyone else, not to me. Casey doesn't smile much, his minute gesture is something he's only given me to let me know we're okay.

"I love you Ava but...you're like a sister to me. And you're dating my brother," Casey says.

We both burst in laughter, breaking the awkward tension. I stand and wrap my arms around Casey's waist, my head resting on his chest. His arms envelop me and I relax. Our friendship means more to me than anything else, and I know all too well how fickle relationships are. Casey knows this too. He's not rejecting me, he's protecting us.

We jump apart when a knock taps my door three times.

"Oh my god, Cole is here," I say. I go to my front door and see the top of his fade through the peep hole. "Casey, what do we do," I whisper. I turn around to Casey disappearing into the back of my apartment, a trail of smoke in his wake. Cole knocks again, I wave my arms frantically to get rid of the remaining vapor. When I'm back at the door, I bring in a deep breath to calm my nerves and open to Cole on the other side with an exhale. Hoping I gave Casey enough time to make it down the fire escape from my bedroom safely.

When Cole raises his head, his entire demeanor is low, sullen. Something has happened—did he look into his parents and discover his twin brother? Cole steps inside slowly, I take his hand in mine as the door closes and we make our way to the couch. I remove his backpack from his shoulders and we collapse together. Cole intertwines our fingers without looking up at me.

"Cole, what's wrong," I ask.

"I got fired today," he says.

My eyes widen. "Oh my god. I'm so sorry."

When he looks at me I try to find more words of solace. I come up short. It's not like I can write his book for him.

"I don't know what else to say. I don't know. I'm sorr—"

He nods discouraged, and my lips close.

"Just...hold me."

I scoot closer to him with open arms, he comes to lay his head on my chest and settles. I place my hand on the nape of his neck and the silence shifts from tense to ease.

"Wait, Ava, you don't smoke."

"What do you—" I stop when noticing Casey's pack of cigarettes on my table. *Fuck!*

I hop off the couch, snatch the carton and toss it in my kitchen trash. On the plus side, Casey's lungs have a reprieve for the day. On the negative, I have to face Cole and attempt to explain away my behavior. Neither of us speaks and no matter what role I'm playing, I won't let anyone believe I smoke or need to inhale, drink or inject to be able to go about my day.

"I don't smoke!" Cole's flinch almost has him covering his ears at my outburst. I don't mean to yell. My heart is beating too fast to cover my truth, and Casey's mistake.

"I know."

"It was a friend's..."

Cole stands and pokes out his bottom lip. "Ok well...I still want to be held."

His childish sulk trumps my fumble. I go to Cole with an idea requiring neither of us to talk for awhile, taking his hand and toward my bedroom.

My eyes were red and the bags underneath were heavy. I couldn't draw myself away from the need to escape. I've been wrecked for eleven days and counting. Sober heartbreak lingers. I remember being with Noah, before he left me, and all the possibilities were endless. Since our break up, I don't have the proper anesthetic to make me feel better. All I've done is cry without an end in view. Where the fuck is Paul?

"Noah was different. He wasn't supposed to treat me this way. Noah was genuine and accomplished—"

"Was he," Blaine said. "You told me he lied to you about losing his job and didn't try as hard as he implied to get another."

I came up from laying on the couch and sat on one cushion. "It was hard for him to find another job because—"

"He was skimming off the top? Yes, I'd imagine. He was not the man he led you to believe he was, and you had the resources for a clean break. You decided to stay until heartbreak. You cannot continue to let men treat you any kind of way because you assume they'll change—are capable of change. Noah hasn't changed. You can."

I shook my head to dismantle Blaine's truth. I can't have another eight months wasted with nothing to show for it.

"No I saw—Noah was going to build me a house and we'd have three kids. Henry would lay under our lemon tree in our backyard during the summer, it—"

"It was a dream, Ava. A fabrication of what you want, not what you have. Nor what you'd have with Noah. You have goals to keep you focused on the future. Focus."

I wiped under my eyes and nose, then reached for a Kleenex from the side table. "What about Noah?"

"Noah is gone. He's left you. Do not kill yourself over the thought of him."

"He said he'd marry me. Who is going to marry me?"

Blaine rose from his chair and knelt in front of me. He took my shaking, soaked hands and waited until I brought my eyes to his.

"You don't need someone to marry. You need someone to love. Love yourself, Ava."

Love myself? Biggest load of crap I've ever heard.

I snap my eyes open to the night and shadows of my room, leaving my past and Noah deep in the recesses of my subconscious. Holy fuck. If Cole's limbs didn't have us latched together, I'd have lurched him off the bed when I came to. My body wanting to come up straight and catch my breath.

Cole is the prettiest sleeper. Who sleeps with a smile on their face? Our heads rest on one pillow and his essence of serenity, allows my heart to settle. He pulls me closer to lay on my chest. Cole is a warm bloodied male who enjoys close contact. I have him between my breasts, arms on my waist and leg between my thighs; as he sleeps peacefully. I'm usually peaceful too, unless I've jump scared out of a dream by a wayward ex. Now, I'm sweating bullets under Cole's weight and my comforter combined.

Shifting to alleviate some of his weight doesn't stir Cole, he's as still as a statue.

My phone buzzes on my nightstand and I stealth reach for it to avoid waking Cole. When Henry falls asleep on me, I make movements just as careful because if I wake him, he'll go sleep on the opposite side of the room—physically telling me 'F you for waking me up, I'd find a new mom if I could.'

My screen lights with a text notification from Casey. It's short enough, I don't have to open my phone.

Casey
you saved us earlier, thank you

I bury the emotions I genuinely have for Cole as he hugs me around my waist. I feel his tongue falling out of his mouth on my skin. I hold my breath against the arousal building between my legs.

He exhales. "I love you, Av..."

What?! I try to squirm to get a look at Cole's face to see if he's awake but his weight pastes me to the mattress and his steady breathing hasn't changed. He's still asleep. And he said he loves me?

No man has ever said they love me first ~~until Mitchell~~. That was always my mistake.

Cole said he loves me. I slap my hand over my mouth to keep from squealing.

He had to have meant me right? Cole could be playing me as I am him. He could have meant 'I love playing you.' Still, he said my name. He almost said my entire name.

Either way, I'm not getting anymore sleep tonight.

Chapter 28
Cole

When I left Speck, I had all the momentum in the world to command Ava tell me what all she is keeping from me. During the long walk to her apartment, I realized there's nothing she can do for me to finish my book. And thinking she owes me anything is weak. She needs time, and the only answer I need is from my main male character Elliot.

Why has he continued developing a connection with a woman he barely knows and caught intense feelings for? What is the shock and awe he looks past in order to stay devoted to her?

I have to wreck my writers brain to uncover what'd make someone stay after hearing their girlfriend's best kept secret.

I stretch my arms and open my eyes to no one else in the bed with me. What I thought was Ava's body was a number of pillows I've got tucked around me.

"Hello," I croak. Nothing. I fight the covers to find my phone and again nothing. No new notifications and nothing from Ava.

I would feel like a one night stand except you don't leave someone at a place you have to come back to. Finishing getting my shirt from yesterday back on, I mosey into the morning light of the living room with my phone to my ear, calling Ava. I hear her phone rattling on the table. When I pick up her cell to cancel my call, her screen appears with a photo of Henry as her background and a text from Blaine waiting in her notifications.

Blaine
i've been missing you. check in

My hand clamps around her device. Who the hell is Blaine and what is his right missing Ava?

Goddammit. Nugget and Gail were right. She is a serial dater, and I'm Boo Boo The Foo—

Before my inner monologue gets the best of me, Ava walks in with to go coffee cups and a bag of what is probably breakfast from the smell of things. She kicks her door closed and notices her phone in my hand.

"What are you doing?"

My eyes land on her bare legs on full display behind the hem the same large T-shirt from last night. Which in turn has me silently begging there are actual pants underneath this morning. I clear my throat and answer her question.

"I was looking for you and called. Why? What's wrong?" *Missing Blaine as much as he's missing you?*

Ava walks forward setting down the bag and cups on her living room table and then takes her phone from me, adding a quick peck on my lips, softening my grip.

I fight the urge to wipe her lies from my mouth.

"Nothing's wrong. Let's have a seat." Ava pushes me onto the couch. She bounces next to me with a bright smile, inter-twining our hands to rest in her lap. Her energy is contagious so I smile back despite my questions.

"Since when are you a morning person," I say. It took me awhile to realize Ava prefers to sleep in past 10am. Hence my 'good morning' texts going unanswered for hours.

"Pssh. Yea right. I just feel good about us," she says. Ava kisses me again, her lips only leaving mine because she can't stop smiling. She doesn't pull away from my orbit. My hand slips between her thighs and on its ascent I'm stopped by the brim of her biker shorts. Thank God. Ava opens her legs wider and I can feel her warmth. The way this morning is headed I won't remember to ask her about Blaine.

Blaine could be someone who hasn't gotten over Ava, except Ava says her ex's have—always have. Blaine must be recent.

"I feel good about us too," I say through a clogged throat of fighting emotions.

"I brought you coffee, er—I mean hot chocolate." She brings one cup from the holder and presents it to me with my name on it, the whip cream oozing out of the lid.

"My favorite," I say.

"I know." She winks, proud of herself. "How do you feel about staying in today—you and me?"

I almost give in to her temptation, sidling closer to me, her breast rubbing against my bicep through her worn T-shirt. I struggle to rewire my brain realizing she isn't wearing a bra. "In a perfect world, yes..."

"But." Her high spirits dip and her head lands on my shoulder.

I kiss her temple. "I have to figure out my manuscript, Ava. I know this story is the one to get me published. I have to put the time in. And time with you can be...distracting."

"Can I read some?"

I've never had a girlfriend who was interested in reading my stories. Ava has asked numerous times to view what I'm working on and even subscribed to my magazine. She's amazing.

Be that as it may, there's a possibility Ava could see herself as the protagonist and not with empathy or admiration. I don't want her to feel attacked in any way before I'm able to defend my story.

"I want you to, maybe soon. Definitely not yet," I say. She reaches for her drink and sets the bag she brought for us on my lap to distribute.

Ava nods and I trust she understands. Then I give her the opportunity to make me the same.

"Ava, who's Blaine," I ask.

My streak of perfect timing continues to fail.

Sophomore year, I told my dad I nicked his Mercedes on our mailbox when pulling into the driveway the previous night. He was shaving at the time. All he heard was 'nick' and 'Mercedes' before he whipped his face to me too fast and too close to the blade. Blood spit from his Adam's apple and I passed out. Entirely too much drama before 8am.

When I brought up Blaine, Ava was taking a drink from her straw mid-swallow. She spurts and chokes down what could have landed on my face. I pat her back forcefully. When she regains her wits, her eyes stay on the floor.

"Why are you...who told you—how do you know about Blaine?"

I tap Ava's hand holding her phone and her latch hardens.

"When I called and picked up your phone, I saw the screen. He said he's been missing you and I thought we were together—"

"We are," she says.

Okay. A good start. "Then why do you need Blaine?"

"I don't need him. He's...Blaine isn't who you think he is. I've known him a long time. He's like a youth leader. Oh God, this is giving cultish, isn't it? Let me start from the beginning." She sets down her cup then shifts to me. "Blaine would visit the foster home and he'd listen to us. We accepted him as a trusted confidant. Some kids grew out of it, I didn't. I still talk to him...sometimes."

Her secret. "So you see a therapist." I didn't mean to sound accusatory when Ava jumps to retort.

"I'm not crazy! It's to have someone to talk to. Talk things through."

"You can't talk to me?" Ava shrugs. I massage one of her shoulders to bring her peace of mind. "Try."

With my other hand, I slide my fingers through hers, linking us together.

"A long time ago, I had bad coping mechanisms and easy access to them. I was really into hallucinogens. Sometimes I was able to manipulate them into seeing what my life would be like if I had the chance to change it. Sometimes it worked, I was married with kids and Henry in the backyard. When it didn't, I would try harder remedies.

"Blaine helped me realize the difference between what I had, what I wanted and what was never mine. It was difficult, and I had to grasp reality before my fantasy...killed me."

Damn. "Are you okay now?"

She doesn't look at me. "For the most part. It's not an addiction. It's a...bad coping mechanism, like I said. Blaine likes to check in under unique circumstances."

I'm finally getting her truth. I tread lightly to keep her talking. "What's the current circumstance?"

"You." When I loosen my fingers, Ava doesn't let me go. "I'd search for vices when another relationship failed; whether waking up to their side of the bed left cold and discarded, skipping out on the check or not hearing from someone for days."

I drop my head at her pointed gaze. "Ah. When I didn't call you...you thought I flaked—"

"You won't break my heart," she says. *She's giving me her heart?* "Right?"

"You're right." I lean in to kiss Ava, my lips landing on her teeth because she's smiling.

"I haven't scared you away," she asks.

I shake my head. This conversation went much better than I imagined. I wish I had something stronger to sip on to loosen up my nerves, I guess steamed chocolate will have to do.

"Because you love me," she says.

Turns out Ava doesn't have any better timing than myself, except while I'm coughing up my hot chocolate she's not rubbing my back to make sure I don't choke to death. She waits for me to right myself and answer her question.

"What are you talkin—what did you say," I ask.

Ava's brightness falls and her face is set in all seriousness. Neither a smile nor blink deters her.

"I asked if you love me," she repeats. "Because you said you did last night. In your sleep."

Not again. My REM state always tells my secrets. I couldn't hide anything from my parents. They'd wait until I fell asleep for me to admit my sins. Like when I had about 20 extra people over junior year when they went out of town for the weekend and I promised no more than five. There was a chip in the marble mantle from Nugget betting himself he could tackle our female quarterback, Lauren Bates. When he charged, she stepped to the side, and his helmet head nicked the shelf.

Or when I said I scored a 1550 on the SAT to be able to join the senior class trip to Aspen. All I needed was a 1400 and I got a 1350. I wanted to get to and from Colorado before telling my parents the truth. It took two plates of Thanksgiving dinner and an itis nap, for me to tell on myself.

I had to learn the importance of truth because lying resulted in staying home Friday nights, for home games, and no chance of dating.

Ava takes her hands from mine and crosses her arms. I attempt to placate her by caressing her cheek with my thumb. She's hard as stone.

I clear my throat to explain. "This isn't the first time my subconscious has spoken out of turn, and he never lies." Her face turns into my hand. "Yes, Ava. I do love you."

Her cheeks soften under my knuckles and her smile is back, mimicking mine.

"Okay," she says.

Ava gets up from the couch and begins to clear the table where neither of us have finished our coffee or seen what's inside the bag. My hunger pales in comparison to Ava not replying 'I love you too.' *Okay?!*

I remain still as she moves around her apartment with a sudden need to clean full cups of coffee and an uneaten breakfast.

"Ava?"

"Yea, Cole," she says from the kitchen.

I can't get up from the couch. *Okay?!*

"Is there anything you'd like to say back to me?" I can't attempt to decipher her eyes or body movements when she's behind the kitchen counter, pilfering around. "I love you, Ava."

Ava comes back into the living room, wiping her hands on a dishcloth.

"I said 'okay.'" Nonchalant.

I remind myself Ava doesn't have any experience with someone loving her and meaning it. I meant it. She needs time to herself to think. I go over to her, rest my hands on her hips, and stand a foot away to keep some distance between us. I've given enough of myself away for the day.

"Okay, I'm going to go home—shower and write."

"We can shower here," she teases.

One of my favorite things about Ava is her presence; around her I always feel lighter. And anytime she offers her time to me I want to immediately take advantage. But right now, I'm unemployed and the woman I love didn't say it back. She and I both need to think about us together and our priorities separate.

"I'll call you," I say.

I kiss her cheek and make my way to her front door. Sliding my backpack on both shoulders I turn around and Ava is still watching me. I can't read her expression beyond satisfaction.

"I love you Ava."

She smiles and waves me off. I wasn't afraid of telling Ava how I feel, I was afraid of what she'd say or do in return. Or not say in return.

What the fuck have I done?

CHAPTER 29
Ava

"Cole loves me."

I'm standing in front of Casey who's looking through me from my couch. He's leaning into his hands, fingers steepled in front of his mouth, thinking to himself. I wait.

"You're positive," Casey asks.

"Casey, Cole told me he loves me."

"What did you say?"

Casey will get a kick out of this. Hell, I did. "'Okay.'"

Casey snickers into his hands. Like I knew he would. It was no trouble playing coy when I got Cole to admit what he said in his sleep, I channeled long lost Enzo.

Enzo was my boyfriend who wine and dined me for a year and a half. In a year and a half, I met his parents, he got an Epipen for his dog allergy—even before Henry, he knew I wanted a dog; and Casey didn't scare him away. 547 days together, Enzo invited me to a staycation weekend at Casa Broad Ripple.

I hadn't seen much of northern Indianapolis as I prefer to walk and don't own a car. It was a whole different scene and I thought Fountain Square was packed; we at least had suitable parking. Our suite was cozy with a fireplace, around the clock room service and a screened in porch.

For three uninterrupted days, Enzo and I were together in front of the fire and underneath a thin blanket. While reminiscing on our long weekend on the way home, I took his hand in mine and told him I loved him. Enzo nodded his head twice, shrugged and said 'okay.'

The rest of the drive was spent in silence until we got back to my house. Done waiting for him to reply, I got out and grabbed my bag from the backseat. I didn't look back at him. I couldn't believe all the time we spent together was for nothing. He needed time. And I could do that for someone I loved.

"Hey, Ava." I turned around to Enzo hanging out of his open window. "I'll call you."

He didn't.

"Good," Casey says, snapping me back to the present. "This is good. He's probably driving himself mad crazy. When you gonna see him again?"

I pick up my phone from the arm of the couch to zero notifications. My face falls a bit, I shrug to Casey.

"He said he'd call."

Casey nods, leans back and lights a cigarette, smiling to himself. I smile too. Under Cole's spell, I always go back to what he and I could be to each other.

No secrets. True feelings. And they all lived—

"What are you doing," Casey says, standing and blowing smoke out the corner of his mouth, analyzing me. "Why are you smiling?"

"I—I'm not."

The scrutiny of his gaze chills me. "Do you like Cole, Ava?"

I scoff and "Pssh" until I find words to make a full sentence. "Believe me Case, it's not like that. He says nice things, I guess. Things I've never heard before. I don't like him, he's not even that cute to be caught up over."

My attempt at humor does nothing to Casey's stone cold face.

"Funny," he says. He comes to stand over me by three inches. I pull my stare from his chest to his eyes. "This is all about us Ava. If we aren't on the same page, then everything we have worked for will have been for nothing. Do you get me?"

"I get you, Casey. There's no need to keep asking me."

"I don't?"

I meet his eyes. "No. You don't."

Casey takes a step back and I let out a quiet breath.

"Good. It's almost time to rip the rug from under him. Just wait. You are his only sense of stability, especially since he lost his job. It won't be adjusting well with him and soon he'll be without the person he claims to love. Sure he has a couple of good friends but I know for a fact they don't compare to his feelings for you. You're destroying him from the inside out. And he'll never recover." Casey's fists are clenched by his sides. "Not without you. That's a uhh...big deal for people."

For Casey not wanting Rayvin to be brought up, he sure references her often.

"Not you," I ask.

"Not us, Ava."

Except Casey had someone he claimed to love once. No one could deny how much Casey and Rayvin meant to each other. He only focuses on his grudge toward her now.

"How..." I fidget and ask, "How different do you think our lives would be if...if things would have worked out between you and Rayvin."

His jaw works side to side. "Rayvin did not love me."

Denial. "We both know she did...she does."

"She doe—you hear from her or something?" He almost sounds optimistic.

Hell no. Rayvin and I couldn't stand each other. What Casey clocked as beauty, I was hesitant. She came in guarded and reserved like the rest of us plus a mission no one else knew about.

I know Casey doesn't think I missed his entire demeanor soften at the thought of Rayvin loving him still.

"She promised she would do anything to make up for what she did," I say. "And she knows the weight those words wield for you."

Casey's features go hard again. He uses his thumb and pointer finger to extinguish the bud of his cigarette without flinching to finish later. "What's your point?"

I groan internally. For a moment I thought Casey would talk to me about his feelings. Mentioning Rayvin shut him away from me and the world again.

I simply shrug in answer to his question. He storms past me and slams the door on his way out.

I don't move from my spot in the middle of the living room. I'm tired of Casey slamming doors, I'm tired of Cole being perfect for someone else, and I'm tired of pretending. I'm freaking tired.

My door opens again and I tense. Casey wraps his arms around me from behind and I slump into his hold.

"I think...let's do something tonight. We're both getting too wound up from all this. Why don't we go out to dinner," he proposes.

My cheeks start to pinch. "Are you asking me out on a date Casey Roberts?"

Casey laughs into my shoulder. We're back. "Ava, will you go to dinner with me?"

I turn around to his front. "What time?"

"7?"

My phone's home screen tells me it's already past six. "That doesn't give me much time."

"I'll wait," he says. Casey kisses me on the cheek and leaves my apartment, closing the door with a quiet click.

I run to my bedroom and pick out an outfit to spend quality time with my best friend.

CHAPTER 30

Casey

"Ava, chill. You're stressing me out. For all anyone knows you are out with your boyfriend."

Since meeting Ava back at her apartment, she has been on pins and needles. Maybe I shouldn't have gotten my new haircut before picking her up, the spontaneity came over me. I went to the barber on my way home and had him shave off my free locs to the same low fade Cole bears.

When I picked her up, I could tell Ava wasn't sure whether or not I was Cole. However, she and I share the same essence: depleted, faux, buried. She has been looking over her shoulder like an inspecting dog, since leaving her apartment.

Ava leans forward, her voice low. "What if my boyfriend recognizes you as my boyfriend or if someone else recognizes you as Cole?"

I shrug with a mouthful of shrimp linguini. "We'll improvise."

Her shoulders refuse to settle and I go back to my plate. No use having my food grow cold waiting for her to loosen up. I add a few more shakes of crushed red peppers and stop with my fork to my mouth when I hear Ava gasp. I feel a hand on my shoulder and retreat to old habits, twisting their hand off me and around their back. I stand and hold their face to the table under my palm. The heavy set red haired man struggles under my hold as I don't let up. Stares from the other patrons sends my anxiety farther north. Shit. The last thing we need is to make more of a scene.

"Cole, what the hell are you doing man," Red Hair spits.

Cole? The majority of my life growing up, I hardly felt a welcome or gentle hand. It was always a push, slap, grab; I learned quickly to never be caught unaware. I let my guard down because I'm out with Ava and now look where we are.

When I look up she stares agape from the man I have pinned down on the table to someone coming up behind me.

I didn't really know how Ava and I would explain if we encountered someone from Cole's life. Indianapolis is a city of over 800,000 people, and almost 10,000 in the neighborhood. How are the odds against us? Before my overreaction continues, Ava begins laughing uncontrollably, louder and louder.

A statuesque beauty, standing at six feet with skin a shade of onyx hidden under a small black dress rounds the table and laughs with Ava. Picking my jaw up from its descend, I join in as well.

"Well well well. You must be our Ava, I'm Gail," Gail says with a broad white smile. She's unnecessarily beautiful: glowing, unblemished skin, pronounced cheekbones, sparkling eyes. And she's with this guy under my hand?

"Are we okay over here," the waiter says, appearing seemingly out of nowhere. He's leaning over to look Nugget in the eye. Nugget raises a thumb skyward.

"You heard him," Gail says.

The waiter takes his suspicions and slowly walks away. The surrounding gawks lessen one by one.

Ava and Gail shake hands. "Nice to meet you...uhm, Gail."

The red head beneath me is struggling to wiggle himself free. "Let me up Cole. I want to meet your girlfriend," he says.

I release him and take a step to the side. He stands up straight and rolls his shoulders.

"Phew. What was that about?" I sidestep his mock punch by reflex. "It was kinda fun though. Hiii-yah!" He mimicks what he thought I did to him. I.e. swinging his arms about. I didn't or have never uttered the words hi-yah.

"Hey, I'm Ava," she says, taking the attention from who I'm supposed to be.

"Call me Nugget," he says. *Nugget?* I thought that was his social media presence. I wouldn't have thought he'd introduce himself by that name. "I'm Cole's right hand man. Thank God he's found a new left."

Nugget winks with a laugh and Ava takes her hand back, wiping her palm on her dress. Gail swats Nugget's arm.

"You're sick," Gail says.

Nugget clasps me on the shoulder, I tense for a fraction of a second before returning to the role of his best friend and smile.

"I thought you ditched because you had an epiphany you had to stay home and write about. Yet you're here," Nugget accuses.

"Ava gave me an offer I couldn't refuse," I say. Good line. I gift Ava a smile for getting us out of my faux pas.

"Strike two Ava," Nugget says, wiggling two fingers in front of his face.

Ava smiles politely.

"Leave her alone. And Nugget is sorry for interrupting," Gail says.

"No I'm not—"

"Cole, we still have to get a game night planned."

"I haven't forgotten," I say.

Gail tugs Nugget out of the restaurant. Ava and I take our seats back and sit in relief.

"You must be doing something right, A. I'm proud of you," I say.

"Yea...right. So, we knew about Nugget," she says, watching the door Nugget and Gail used to leave the restaurant.

I shake my head with a scoff. "Nugget...I thought his name was an inside joke. I never thought he'd actually introduce himself as such."

"I didn't know about Gail. Did you?"

Ava says Gail's name with a pinch of distaste and an ounce of envy. She saw what I did. One of the most gorgeous women I've ever laid eyes on and she spends her free time with Cole. Ava wouldn't be able to hold a candle to a rival like Gail.

"Green isn't a good color on you," I sing.

She snaps her eyes to me. "I'm not jealous."

My face says she's as transparent as glass.

"Shut up," she says, rolling her eyes, taking her glass of wine to chug like water.

Upon getting back into Ava's apartment she goes straight to the couch and lands face first. I believe her food coma has taken her under until she rolls over. With only the oven light shining from the kitchen, I can't make out her features. The familiarity we've built brings me comfort.

"I. Am. Stuffed."

"I'm glad you had a good time," I say, stabilizing myself on the arm of the couch.

"We need to do this again," she says.

I know Ava has missed me. I've missed her too, still, the knowledge of my birth family is bigger than either of us or the time we've shared throughout our lives. I don't think we properly calculated how much time apart this would keep us.

"Yea, once it's done," I say.

I rise to head back to our house when Ava catches my hand.

"Casey, will you stay the night? We can finish the night with hooky. Please. Tomorrow I'll be Cole's girlfriend again. Tonight I want to be *your* best friend."

She doesn't give me much time to debate her, pulling me down on the couch, begging with batting eyelashes.

"Okay," I groan. Its been almost six months apart. One night together won't kill us.

Ava claps twice, gets up from the couch, and heads down the hall to her bedroom. I remove my jacket and rest my head against the back of the sofa.

She returns dressed in pajamas, braids tucked in her bonnet, and her hands behind her back. I know exactly what she's hiding.

"Ava, no. Not again," I plead.

She ignores me and goes to the DVD player to put in her favorite movie: the black *Cinderella*, starring Brandy and our late great Whitney Houston. Both of us can quote this movie from start to finish. Ava saw it once at Miss Green's and we've barely seen any other movie since she found a pirated DVD online.

The machine whirs and the television comes to life. Ava comes back with a bottle of wine and two glasses.

"It's a classic," she says.

Ava fills each glass and slides back into the couch, handing me one.

"Cheers," I say.

CHAPTER 31
Ava

I fell asleep on the couch during the third re-watch of Brandy's *Cinderella*. Every re-watch, there's a different part I look forward to seeing/singing. I remember muttering the lyrics to the "Stepsisters Lament" before my eyes closed for the night.

When I wake up, the sun is shining bright through my blinds and I bring the cover I'm wrapped in over my head.

Speaking of my head, it's fuzzy and heavy. Casey and I shared two bottles of wine last night and maybe if the totality wasn't equivalent to the price of two kids meals, I wouldn't be waking up with a hammering headache and dry mouth. I peek out of the cover and look around for Casey. He's not in my immediate vicinity, so I decide to hide back under my blanket until he gets back.

As my mouth is going slack, I hear my front door open.

"Ugh, you besta have coffee," I say.

"How'd you know," Cole asks.

"Cole?!"

I pop up from the couch and am confronted with the aroma of last night's red wine wafting throughout my apartment. My eyes adjust to Cole standing in my living room. He sets our usual coffees on the table then raises my legs to lay on top of his as he makes himself comfortable. Slowly, I lie back down, taking deep breaths to curb the nausea swimming in my brain and stomach.

"Expecting someone else," he asks, leaning over to kiss me on my lips.

I blink my eyes open, my lips pursed for more. "Of course not. I didn't know you were stopping by." I peek over at my phone on the edge of the table for the time. *7am?!* "And so early."

"I thought I'd surprise you. I have a lot more time on my hands now."

Time he wants to spend with me. "I'm flattered."

I rise carefully from the couch to clear the table of empty wine glasses and bottles. When I return Cole hands me my iced caramel macchiato.

"What did you get into last night," he asks.

"Nothing." I take my first swig. "Mmm, that's the stuff."

"You had two wine glasses out."

Fuck. "Oh. Oh yea. I caught up with a friend I haven't seen in a while."

Cole mocks a spit take and wipes his mouth with the back of his hand. "Ava, you have friends?!"

I shove him away. "Not many. It wasn't anything important." My throat clogs in retaliation. Casey's and I friendship is the of utmost importance. I wouldn't be here otherwise.

He places a hand on my knee, all serious now. "I'd be happy to meet the people you grew up with."

"Be careful what you wish for," I mumble under another sip.

Cole massages my leg and the bud of my center tingles at the brewing possibilities. He brings his lips to mine and I let him remove my coffee from my grip to follow his lead moving us to lay together along the couch. We're heady breaths, moans, and hands until my stomach announces its distress. Last night's gumbo and wine combination are not digesting well together.

I push Cole off me.

"What's wrong?"

I catch my gag with my hand and run to my bathroom toilet. I wrench once and last nights drinks and dinner splatter the toilet bowl. All of a sudden my shirt feels like it's shrinking, clinging to my sweaty back. The only remedy is my cheek against the chill of the toilet seat. While waiting between dry heaves and wet mouth, Cole knocks.

"Ava?"

I reach for the door behind me to slam closed just for it to bounce open again. "Cole, please leave. I'll text you later."

This is humiliating. I hang my head in the silence following his departing steps. Except, Cole returns placing a damp paper towel to the back of my neck. I relax while also knowing it's not over yet. Vomiting, dry heaving, and flush in five minute intervals. When I'm only retching, I rest my head on my hand hanging on the rim of the toilet.

Before I fall asleep, Cole scoops me up in his arms and carries me to my bed. He tucks me in, adds another cold cloth to my forehead and kisses me on the cheek.

"Want me to get you anything," he asks.

My arm is to weak to make my way to cradle his cheek, landing on his chest. "You put me in bed."

"I didn't know how long laying over the toilet would be a proper resting place for you."

I reach both arms up and he wraps his around me. "Thank you," I say in his ear.

He kisses my cheek again. "I'll call you later."

"Okay," I whisper, releasing him before sleep gets the best of me.

"I love you."

Even though Cole may be out of my league presently, he's exactly the guy I would concoct for myself in real life. And the haunting reality is, the more I wake up as Cole's girlfriend the sooner I won't be.

I feel a dip in my bed and I smile involuntarily. Cole's back. I roll over to his mouth set in a thin line, the rest of his features just as harsh. Oh no. Has Cole found out about Casey? My throat constricts until noticing the darkness held in his eyes. Casey's eyes. My break is short lived. Casey is in my room, on my bed and hardened by the weight of the world on his shoulders. I jump and bring my cover up to my chin.

"Casey, what are you doing here—"

"Stop leaving your door unlocked. What happened earlier," he asks.

"First of all, *you* left my door unlocked. Where were *you* this morning?"

"Answer *me*, Ava."

"I don't even know what you're talking about."

"This morning—are you sick?"

Oh. Why doesn't he start caring instead of hostile.

Casey carefully puts the back of his hand on my forehead. I don't feel as special compared to Cole's caresses, but I'm so tired I do relax a little. I turn my head and his hand falls. I pull myself up to lay against my headboard.

"Wine and gumbo don't mix," I say. His eyes don't shift.

All this morning was was too much wine, not enough bread. There's nothing more to tell so I don't know what he's waiting for.

"Okay," he says. Casey gets up and leaves my bedroom. I hear the front door open and close then lay back in need of at least another hour or two of rest.

I couldn't go back to sleep until mid afternoon. Which then resulted in me sleeping the day away. So when Cole texted to spend the night watching movies, I accepted without a hint of hesitation.

As I was willing to go to the corner store for snacks, Cole assured me he'd bring the necessities for the night. He entered my apartment with a full brown paper bag tucked under his arm, and donning a checkered onesie. Putting my oversized T-shirt and sweats to shame.

His only condition for our movie night was we have to watch his favorite movie first. Like Casey, I've made Cole watch the black *Cinderella* with me plenty of times so I have no problem granting his request—once.

With Cole close and only the blue light from the TV, I look over his features again before looking at the menu screen. With Casey's new haircut, I've been having to do a double take to make sure I know who I'm really with.

Cole presses play on *The Parent Trap* and my stomach dips.

"*The Parent Trap*," I ask.

"Don't laugh. It's a classic," he says.

This has got to be a joke. "Your favorite movie is not *The Parent Trap*. You're playing me. And I thought you didn't play games Cole Roberts." I cross my arms and roll my neck.

"This is my favorite movie, Ava."

His unwavering stare makes me drop my teasing.

"Why," I ask.

Cole shrugs and leans forward to unload the grocery bag of apple juice and saltine crackers. What kind of movie food is this?

"I didn't want to upset your stomach," he says with a wink and I melt.

I snatch the crackers from the table and hold them close to my chest.

Cole pouts at my most prized possession. "Maybe I didn't think this through. Those are in my spot."

Oh damn. I open my arms to him and we settle into the couch to watch Cole's favorite movie, which is ironically close to his real life. If he only knew.

By the end of the movie, I'm now wrapped in Cole's bare arms. The top half of his onesie bunched at his waist. As the credits are rolling, he wraps me against him and kisses my hair.

We linger in silence before Cole asks, "Do you have any siblings?"

I scaugh—half scoff, half laugh. "No."

The way Cole is holding me, I feel something is about to happen and I'm racking my brain to prepare for the worst.

"What if you had to guess," he says.

I've thought about my biological family long enough to know exactly how to phrase this answer. "Absolutely not. Somehow I was able to slip through the cracks—literally and figuratively. My birth mom was a dancer, an exotic dancer, and was apart of the extras involved."

Cole thinks. "Drugs?" I don't say anything. "Did she have to...did she have a—"

"Most likely." Whether he was going to ask about a John, selling or using, my mom had a hand in it all.

"I'm sorry," he says.

"Don't be." I slip out of his arms and hold my head in my hands. My braids blocking Cole from seeing me.

I'm not sorry my mom abandoned me. I'm not sorry I don't have a single example for stability—no matter how hard I fight for it. I'm not sorry I continue to chase a dream always leaving me empty and heartbroken.

I repeat each sentence to myself to build me up and yet, a single tear still escapes, proving I'm weak.

Cole reaches for me and I move to the other side of the couch. I need a minute.

"I had a brother," he says.

What? I snap my head to Cole, his hands now holding his head, blocking himself from me.

"How did you know," I blurt.

He looks up with water rimmed eyes. "What?"

God damnit. I can never think before speaking. I almost brought up Casey and their impossible parents. Instead, I take Cole's hand in mine and caress gently.

"What do you mean by *had*," I ask with caution. When I felt something happening, I didn't think it was Cole knowing about Casey—knowing *something* about Casey. Cole is finally about to tell me everything I need to know. I'll have Casey off my back. Then Cole and I will have a fair chance to begin mending what's broken when the truth is out in the open.

"He died during childbirth. I was born first, he didn't make it. I was a twin...Am I still? Are you still considered a twin when one didn't make it?" I shake my head, failing to grip what Cole is saying. *Died during childbirth?!* "Unfortunately, he was strangled by the umbilical cord."

What?! "Who told you that?"

"My parents."

Strangled by the—It's taking the strength of the Incredible Hulk to reel in my anger and the truth. He doesn't know. "Your parents told you your twin brother died?"

Cole snatches his hand out of mine and his eyes pierce me with such resentment. Eyes I've seen on his brother all my life.

"That's what happened," he says.

He's upset. He doesn't know. For the last year Cole's been an orphan. Casey has been abandoned since birth and his parents told Cole this bullshit?! I wait a beat before I continue.

"So you grew up an only child," I ask.

Cole nods. I dig my finger nails into my palm to keep from shaking him. *Speak!* I need more!

"Yes. I've always missed the opportunity of growing up with a brother. I spent my birthdays with twice as many candles wishing for another bro—any sibling," he says.

"And?"

Cole shakes his head and wipes under his eyes before pointing to the screen with a fond smile. "But *The Parent Trap*—classic! I always imagined my brother and me getting into mischief and mayhem. Pulling it off way better than Hallie and Annie—nothing against women or anything." He winks and gives me a nervous smile.

I laugh, nervous as well. "I understand now."

The question is, will Casey?

I'm looking up at Casey from the couch waiting for him to say something. I told him exactly what Cole said to me last night and he's been standing with clasped hands at his mouth deliberating.

"Do you believe him," he asks.

I swallow hard. "I believe it's what his parents—*your* parents—told Cole."

He drops his hands. "Do you believe Cole, Ava?"

I stand. "How could you not?"

"Because it's bullshit!"

"I know!"

"Strangled." Casey scoffs. "I wasn't 'strangled.' My parents didn't want me." His voice breaks as he fights off tears. "Our parents shouldn't have said anything if they couldn't come up with a better lie. I. Have. Been. Here. Right here!"

"Casey, I know—Cole doesn't. Your parents completely misled him. Cole is...he's innocent."

Casey's body tenses and I know all he can see is red. Fuck. He's not breathing. He's so pissed he's not breathing and I'm preparing myself for the fallout from my fumbled words. As he clenches his fists open and close, I make a vow to think before I speak.

"Innocent," he fumes. "*I* am innocent! Since when have you not known that?"

Casey waits for me to recognize and I do, I always have. He needs to recognize Cole is not the enemy.

"Casey, you're not with Cole the way I am. You don't need to blame him—"

"Well I do. I do blame him. He could have done something," Casey says, a tear slipping down his cheek.

"Like what?"

"Research! Because I did and I found out my parents had two children and they—they only kept one...they kept Cole while I got left, to be abused and dismantled for years—"

"I know Casey. I was there. I've been there," I say. "Listen, I think now is a good time to stop this charade. This is what you needed. The truth. You have it. Cole needs his brother. It's not too late."

Casey wipes his face with his sleeve and looks me dead in the eye. "What's too late is you being able to keep your promise to me. You're like everyone else."

"*What?!*" After everything I've done for him. My feelings and time be damned. I would not still be with Cole as a make believe girlfriend if I wasn't on Casey's bandwagon. He can't discredit me when I'm uprooting my life and sanity. I'm doing everything I can and all I get is pieces of answers that are never good enough.

Casey makes his way to the front door. I get there first to block his exit. We are the only people we have. I can't let him leave.

"I don't like this Ava."

"Me neither."

Casey takes a step back and looks me in the eyes. "You are supposed to be on my side. This is the one time I need you. You promised...and I'm not getting the same respect. Please move."

Now I'm crying. I bite my bottom lip to keep my voice from cracking. "Where are you going?"

His eyes meet the floor. "I don't know. I need some air."

Casey reaches around me for the door knob and I press my back harder against his exit.

"Casey, you can't. I need you to be okay." Casey pulls on the handle, digging into my lower back. I stand strong against my wince. "Stop. You don't—we don't run away from each other. I'm sorry."

I wrap my arms around Casey's neck and pull him down to me, my hand caressing the crop of his fade. I hold him until he releases the doorknob and wraps me in his arms.

"I need you Ava. No one else can help me."

I use all my strength to bind us. "I'm here."

CHAPTER 32
Cole

The opportunity Nugget and Gail have been hoping for is finally here. Tonight is game night: Nugget and Gail versus Ava and myself.

Ava left her front door unlocked for me to enter her apartment and has yet to come out of her bedroom dressed and ready to go. I've been glued on her couch for twenty minutes.

I came early for cuddles and kisses not to help Ava choose what outfit she should wear. Since I'm in Adidas sweatpants and a T-shirt, I thought I set the bar low. Ava is giving this occasion more credit than it deserves.

"Ava, game night is not a big deal. I promise," I yell for my voice to travel to her bedroom.

Ava peeks around the corner with a long sleeve sweater against her chest. "Cole, this interrogation could make or break us. Friends are important."

She goes back and comes out dressed in skinny jeans and a sleeveless top, paired with her always worn pair of Converse and a cropped denim jacket. I get up from the couch, meet her in the middle of the room, and finally hold her in my arms.

"That's why it's time for you to meet mine. Nugget and Gail can be a smidge territorial," I say.

Ava swings out of my arms. "Why didn't you tell me that earlier. They already must hate me. I'm screwed. I've gotten to like you all this time for nothing when Gail and—do you really call him Nugget?" I snort. When someone eats $80 worth of chicken nuggets a week to bulk up for summer football tryouts and still doesn't make the team; he deserved some credit. "Gail and Nugget will rip me to shreds."

I didn't compute anything after Ava admitted she likes me.

"Ava, I love you. Nugget and Gail are important to me and I want them to know I'm in good hands."

I pull her chin to release her teeth from bearing down on her bottom lip. My thumb sweeps along the edge and I lean in to kiss her.

She thinks again. "Do we have to go all the way to Nugget's? I know how much time you spend at The Falcon, we could go there. Then I'd be able to excuse myself to the 'bathroom' and actually run upstairs and hide in the back corner of your closet until they leave."

Ava has been impulsive and wonderous. I've yet to see her panic. Seeing her frazzled at the thought of losing me is endearing. She doesn't have anything to doubt. I'm not going anywhere, I'm hers.

"Nugget and Gail are going to love your humor, lets go." I smack her butt and she marches to the front door then stops. I round to face her, taking her by the arms. "Ava, are you going to be okay?" Her head drops to my chest with a nod. "Should we have a code word in case things get weird?"

She looks up with playful eyebrows. "Like what?"

I tap my chin. "How about—"

"Yahtzee—hell yea!" Nugget pumps his hands in the air upon his third victory and fifth cup of Gail's vodka punch.

"How the fuc—again?! I know you two are cheating and when I find out how, your ass is grass," I threaten.

Gail scoffs. "My ass is grass? How old are you Grampa?"

"Grampa?" I look at Ava. She's been quiet throughout the night but calm. "People don't say 'ass is grass'...anymore?"

Ava shrugs. "I've only haven't heard the phrase for about a week or so," she teases.

I pull her into my side and kiss her temple.

"Last week wasn't the 80's Ava," Nugget says. "If you're gonna stay around, you'll have to call Cole out on his shit."

I scoot our chairs closer and land my arm around her shoulders, trailing my fingers up and down the goosebumps along her bicep. "She'll be around."

Ava turns her head to mine and I can't help myself from bringing my mouth to hers.

"I knew they loved each other," Nugget says. Gail elbows him in the stomach and he keels over. "Ah, damn! What did I say?"

Ava jumps out of my hold, my arm falling down the back of her chair. The uncomfortable stillness stretches while we avoid the others eye contact.

"How about another game," Gail suggests.

Four new pairs of cards are dealt among us to set up a new game. Ava's eyes are fastened to the stack in her hands. I look to Nugget and he mouths 'I'm sorry.' I shake off his condolences. It's not his fault.

Ava pulls her arms through the sleeves of her jacket and crosses them in front of her chest. Nugget and Gail walk us to the front door with forced smiles.

"Thanks for coming over you two. Y'all have fun," Gail asks.

"We did," I answer for us both and give Gail a hug. I can barely hear Nugget while we're embraced, when Ava pulls me away.

"Ava, good to see you ag—"

"Ready to go," Ava says.

She intertwines her fingers in mine then pulls slightly. "Yea. We'll see you guys later." I narrow my eyes to Nugget on our way out and he shrugs. I have to remember to bring it up later to catch up on what I missed. "Thanks again."

"Okay, see ya," Nugget says.

We leave them to the cleaning up of numerous board games and half empty glasses.

The night breeze feels good against the flush of my cheeks. I'm thinking about how well tonight went, excluding Nuggets faux pas. I'm sure the four of us could make wonderful memories together. Nugget has never blatantly noticed my feelings for my partner and spoke on it. I'm happy for my friends to see me happy with Ava.

"I like your friends," Ava says.

"Yea—"

"Nugget is really funny. And Gail is really pretty," she says.

"You know, sometimes I don't even pay attention to what Nugget says—" *Wait.* "Gail? What about Gail?"

"She's pretty. Are you two close?"

I stop walking and bring Ava in front of me, my eyes boring into hers to prove I'm serious.

"It's me, Gail and Nugget. Never me and Gail. Okay?"

Ava steps out of my hold. "You expect me to believe Gail chose to be with Nugget instead of you?"

My head falls. Ava has a bold assumption about my best friends and an even better one of me. It took me an enormous amount of time before I could even look Gail in the eye. Her immediate beauty kept me hushed and flushed for months before she literally slapped it out of my head. I couldn't look at her like a potential contestant on *Americas Next Top Model* from that point on. Gail and Nugget, on the other hand, fit together whether as friends or a dysfunctional couple because of who they are, not what they look like.

"Yea, he makes Gail laugh," I say.

"You make me laugh," she says.

"You think I'm funny?"

"Of course I do."

I wrap my arm around her shoulder and we continue down the street. "You must like me a lot then."

"So did I pass the friends test," she asks.

"With flying colors."

Ava brings her arm around my waist. "Are you sure?"

"I had a code word with them too."

"And I passed?"

"Of course you did," I say. "Who wouldn't love you?"

We decide on an Uber to avoid walking crooked all the way back and get in the car. I hold Ava's hand against my leg, using the ride to find the nerve to ask her something important.

When we get out of the car at her building, my heart hammers to get this out before we reach her door. Getting past the threshold before, doesn't automatically grant me access each time. I take the plunge when we're coming up the staircase from the third floor hand in hand.

"Ava, next Saturday..."

"What's next Saturday," she asks, as my sentence hangs.

"Next Saturday is our six month anniversary," I say.

Her eyes widen. "Six months?"

"Six months from the day we had our first date at the diner." We both smile at the memory of our first date night. Then our faces scrunch, cringing at how we left the diner. I always had an inkling Ava could be important to me, I'm precarious if she's aware how much after all this time.

"Hmm."

She slips her hand from mine and walks ahead of me.

Hmm? This woman, I tell you what. "Ava, I want us to celebrate. I was thinking going to the same diner from our beginning, Heather's?"

"HA! You think they'll remember us?"

I catch her hand before she gets out her keys, whipping her into my chest. Her gasp bout undoes me. "I'll be sure to pay this time." Our breaths continue to mix. "Date night? Saturday? Yes?"

Her eyelashes bat as quick as her breaths. "I'll see you Saturday, Cole."

My smile takes hold slowly and lean into her lips for her to slip from my grasp. She closes the door to her apartment, leaving me on the other side; similar to how we started six months ago.

CHAPTER 33
Cole

No matter the amount of time I take to breathe deeply, I cannot calm down. My nerves are on overdrive. I see Matt through the window of Bovaconti and try to find my nerve before crossing the street to join him. I find a pinch of reprieve with clear eyes and set goals—Matt accepting my manuscript for publication, Matt putting me back on payroll—and forge ahead to present myself in front of my previous boss at the table he's chosen.

When he sees me headed toward him, he stands with his hand out to shake. "Cole good to see you—"

I slam my manuscript in front of him. "This is business."

Matt brings my novel closer and sets his magnetic readers on the bridge of his nose. "Let's get started then."

He flips the cover page and begins; putting an end to my over confident facade. It's hard to keep my knee still, waiting for him to get through enough words to tell me I can come back to Speck.

"Cole, your shaking is distracting. How about you go get us some coffee," Matt says, without looking up.

"We don't drink coffee."

"Then get my tea and your chocolate."

"Of course." I jump out of my chair and my legs bump the table. Matt holds on to the sides to steady the pages of my manuscript.

"Sorry," I say.

He waves me off. "Go."

I leave him hunched over my manuscript, shoulders threatening to bust out of his polo; and go to the counter to order my hot chocolate and Matt's preferred green tea from Joe. I can't look back no matter how much I want to.

"Long time no see," Joe says, cleaning his eyeglasses with his shirt, then situating them on the bridge of his nose.

"I know. I know. Been working."

"Anything good?"

"That's why I'm here." I send my thumb over my shoulder. "My boss is reading my story. Green tea and hot chocolate please."

"Tea, iced?"

"Yea," I say.

When Joe takes our drinks from the passing barista and sets them in front of me, I whisper, "How does he look—is he bored?"

He looks over my shoulder and shrugs. "He's reading."

"Any reactions?"

His eyes cut over me, then back. "No, he's still."

"How still?"

Another quick eye shift. "Statue."

My head falls. "Shit."

Joe waves me away when I reach for my wallet. "On the house." Then his eyes widen. "He stopped reading."

"There's no way." I whip to Matt—who's on the phone! I turn back and slam my head on the counter. "Are you guys hiring?"

Joe taps me on the shoulder and nudges the cups to me. I rise and take our drinks back to the table.

I slump into my chair. "You didn't read enough."

Matt doesn't look up from his phone. "Didn't have to."

He can't even give me the respect to look me in the eye as he trashes my career, my livelihood. If I'm not writing, I'm nothing. There is nothing else in the world I could ever succeed in. I'm a writer—a novelist. This novel has the ability to make readers feel beyond boy meets girl and the thought of starting from scratch makes me...

"Cole, this is brilliant," Matt says.

The dark cloud around me that was so close to swallowing me whole, starts to brighten. Matt comes into view with a wide smile.

"What," I ask. "I mean, you barely read—"

"I needed the meat and you found it." Matt is giving me his full attention, phone put away. "I have chills."

"Seriously?"

Matt stands, tucking my first novel headed toward publishing under his arm.

"Come in Monday morning and we'll talk deadlines. Enjoy your weekend and welcome back," Matt says, sticking out his hand to shake.

I meet him standing and accept his hand, his offer. He has chills.

I'M. GETTING. PUBLISHED.

Thankfully Matt already left before seeing me pumping my fists in the air, resulting in my hot chocolate burning me through my clothes. I give a shy smile to the remaining customers, wipe myself up and remember the last time I had coffee spilled all over me.

Ava.

I wasn't chagrined today or six months ago because each time something new came into my life, leading me into a new adventure.

Six months after meeting the woman I now love, my debut novel is moving forward to publish. How did I get so lucky?

CHAPTER 34

Casey

My breaths rush out of me like a caged bull watching Cole. He's happy as can be, even spilling coffee all over himself like a dunce doesn't simmer his glee. Matt must have given him good news and the last thing Cole deserves is another brand of good fortune I never received.

Even with his stupid book from his small publishing house, Cole won't stand a chance without Ava.

I stomp away from the coffee shop and toward Ava's apartment. I let myself in without knocking and she jumps up off the couch.

"Casey?"

Ava wipes her face where Hot Cheetos dust coats the edge of her mouth and combs through the section of hair where she's removed a third of her braids.

"Did you know Cole got his job back," I ask.

Ava is usually quick to answer any question I have about Cole. I'm not stupid enough to believe she hasn't acquired real feelings for him and she's not stupid enough to break her promise to me. The fact that she's not hurrying to tell me all about Cole's project while fighting to gush how proud of him she is, brings me up short. Of course Cole wouldn't tell Ava everything as he's cut from the same cloth of his parents and myself.

"Uhm, he was working on something—totally convinced he'd get published...he never let me read anything though," she says, fixing all her hair in one ponytail.

I mull that over for a moment. Cole didn't let Ava read his book but was pretty much skipping when she subscribed to his magazine. Ava has read his posts online and in print from Speck Publications. Now, when he's publishing his first novel, he leaves Ava clueless?

My blood boils thinking this is how he treats his girlfriends as well. Leading someone on, dangling them by the hook... Come hell or high water, Ava will be leaving him first. Being left by the one you love is worse than leaving who you love.

As I've been wounded since Rayvin, she's been lost since me. She used me, I left her. Rayvin's only goal is redemption, making it easy for her to bend to my will. Why else has she been hassling me for another chance?

Cole will soon be putty in Ava's hands—doing the exact thing I will him to do.

"Well, you still mean a lot to him...for now," I say.

"Is it time?"

"We're really close."

"How close," she asks.

I laugh to myself. "Do you have plans Saturday?"

Ava covers her mouth with a gasp. I give her a wink and leave. Neither Cole nor Ava are ready for what I have planned, but I am.

CHAPTER 35
Casey

Speck is small. It's on the sixth floor of a high rise building. There's a view but their company doesn't even reach across the entire floor to enjoy it. Their cubicles are little—barely enough room for arms to stretch or chairs to swivel, and half don't have a name tag so most are for show. I grew up in a foster home and I know more room.

My button up shirt is choking the life out of me when I walk upon Cole's old—new—desk. I thought it might be nice for a closer look into Cole's work life, and I couldn't come in dressed in my all black when Cole is prone to loud patterns and graphic T-shirts. I fight my collar for a little more breathing room while taking a gander around the other empty spaces.

"Cole?"

I turn around too fast, ripping my collar an inch. Matt, Cole's boss, stands up from his office chair and comes around his desk to lean against the door frame.

"Hey, Matt."

"I thought we agreed on Monday," he says.

"We did. Yea—we did. I wanted to make sure I still had my same desk."

"I knew you'd be back. I always believed in you, Cole. Never forget."

I have a sudden urge to vomit on all of the privilege Cole's been granted throughout his life. I excelled in math and computer science and never received a gold star sticker or 'good job' handwritten in the corner of tests or homework.

I've never been appreciated. Cole makes up fake people doing fake things and everyone believes in him.

I swallow around the enormous lump I can't pass. "Thanks, Matt. Can't wait to come back Monday."

Matt nods and exits his office, heading towards the restroom. I look around to all the hump back writers in their compact cubicles.

I move quickly to Matt's office, snatch Cole's manuscript from his desk and tuck it into my jacket. Then I take the stairs two at a time to exit.

Matt didn't have a clue I wasn't Cole. I've seen Cole and noticed immediate differences between us and not even his best friends were able to tell us apart.

When Gail and Nugget ambushed our dinner, I had to interrupt them here and there to get their bouts of Ava off their chest. And it has worked. Neither were none the wiser.

Walking into The Falcon, I make my way to the chipped green door in the back corner until I realize I won't be able to get through. I give up for now, passing the bar to leave.

"Cole!"

I stop in my tracks at the animated brunette woman leaning over the bar. Her name tag says 'Sarah.'

"Hey Sarah!" I try to give her the same amount of energy. It makes me sick.

"You forgot your keys again, didn't you?" She leans over the counter her chest coming together almost spilling out of her V-neck top.

I'm going to assume Sarah is in tip mode and not actually giving herself access at a chance with my brother. Cole has the magnetism women respond to. I didn't know I had the same universal charm until I cut my hair from my face and stood up straight. I get second glances from women and a smile in greeting while passing others on the street. It's nice.

Sarah reaches below the bar, bringing out a set of keys on a ring. She shuffles through them before offering me an aged bronze key.

"You're the best Sarah," I say, and take the key to unlock the corner door.

"You always say that," she says.

Hmm. Cole does in fact have advantages I never thought I could have for myself—friends, colleagues who want to see him succeed, bewitching himself out of situations. Maybe if I look the part, the act will follow.

I salute Sarah in thanks and make my way up the stairs to my brothers apartment.

I brought myself here, to Blaine. Even though it was my idea, I can't cushion my posture. This is the first appointment where I've felt valiant because I'm another day closer to the world righting itself.

"Nice haircut," he says.

"I called Rayvin."

Blaine's eyes bug before transferring back to blasé wonderment. "Okay...," he says, leaning back into his chair, propping his left leg on his right knee.

"What?"

"You make it sound like no big deal."

"It can't be," I say.

"What do you mean 'it can't be?'"

"I meant to say it's not a big deal, me calling Rayvin. I'm sure we all knew it was bound to happen sooner or later."

"I didn't know," Blaine says. "Rayvin hurt you Casey. Not only your heart, your body too. I know you love her but there are somethings love can't overcome."

My breathing escalates when Blaine doesn't use past tense. Rayvin being the only woman I ever loved, doesn't translate to mean I feel the same way now. No. I don't.

"Casey?" My eyes cut to Blaine. "You talked to Rayvin. Its been seven years, why?"

"I need her help."

"With what?"

I take a deep breath in and exhale through my nose. "I need someone there for me."

"What about Ava," Blaine asks.

"I don't want to take her away from her boyfriend."

"Ava and Cole have been together for a while."

I nod. "About six months." We both know this.

"And you haven't driven him away?"

"Pssh. I'm not worried about Cole."

"Are you worried about Ava?"

I didn't know I was, or should be, until recently. Blaine always knows the right questions to ask, bringing me up short. The last six months will be for naught if Ava doesn't follow through. All she has to do is break Cole's heart; make him fall into an endless pit of despair due to losing someone he loves. Easy.

"I don't want Ava to forget about what I've done for her without asking for anything in return because—"

"You love her," Blaine says.

I roll my eyes, missing my free locs to hide behind. I don't love Ava. I do not love Ava. She's been my best friend for over 20 years. What we have is well beyond something as basic as love.

I did love Rayvin and there is not many people who doesn't know how well that turned out. We made the local news.

I shake my head. "I can't love Ava. Not the way she needs to be."

"Why?"

"The people I love...it's not reciprocated. The people I love, love other people."

"Ava is of the same mindset about her own failed experiences."

I rub my hands down my face. "No, the people she loves, leave. Not because they don't love her, because they are weak—easily manipulated—"

Placing both feet on the ground, he comes forward, "Easily manipulated by whom?"

I swallow rocks. "What I mean is no one has ever fought for Ava. Whatever they were up against was stronger than their feelings for her. She and I are not the same," I say.

"What happened between you and Rayvin was a long time ago. You said you called her." I nod. "When you called her to be there for you again, what did she say?"

"Anything you need." I try to make my voice sound like the low rasps of Rayvin's I'll always remember.

"Hmm. She's made heavy promises before, no," Blaine says, bursting my bubble.

"I know...I also know she won't risk losing me again."

After talking with Blaine, calling Rayvin to meet face to face could be a huge mistake. However, I have to be prepared for what's out of my control. I don't want anything to go awry that could have been avoided because I didn't ask for help.

"To Cole for getting his job back, me for getting my woman back and...and..."

"Not every toast has to be three fold," Gail says. God damn, that woman is fucking gorgeous; and completely oblivious to the amount of stares she receives tucked under Nugget's fat arm. Love is blind.

Cole raises his shot glass higher, "To us!"

Cole, Nugget—idiot—and Gail clink their glasses together and knock the shots back.

I watch my brother laugh and converse with his friends, none of them with a clue life as they know it will soon never be the same again.

I'm across the bar tucked away in my own booth and absolutely no one has noticed me as Cole's twin brother under my low beanie. I've never understood why people don't look out to see every angle of their present rather than looking down to their phone or thinking off to their next task.

Cole's never seen me walking alongside him on the opposite side of the street. Nugget and Gail should have noticed I was eating lemon garlic shrimp pasta and considered Cole's allergies when they caught Ava and I out. They never looked twice when I was pretending. Matt has yet to call Cole in a frenzy for another copy of his manuscript. Even then, Cole won't have his laptop. They should have known I wasn't Cole, if only they'd look.

I've even almost tricked Ava longer than a few seconds except the bond between us can't shield me for long.

I'm at the Falcon where Cole is known by name and presence, and not a single person has given me a double take. I'm wearing a hat pulled low, not prosthetic enhancements. Sarah didn't even look up from her notepad when she came by to take my order. If Cole were to go to the bathroom and I showed up, his so called 'best friends' would be none the wiser.

Cole's rewarding childhood not altering his outlook on life, his fitted T-shirts and jeans makes him come off as warm, inviting, and unassuming; whereas I drape myself in clothes black and baggy. Its always been my way to hide from everything and everyone. I see Cole with a full smile, loud laugh and great expectations for his future, he's tickled pink. If only he knew what was coming for him.

"Where's Ava," Gail asks. I freeze and try to zone out the chatter throughout the bar and focus on the three seated by the window.

Cole shrugs. "Not sure."

I know where Ava is. I'd bet she's curled up on her couch singing both Brandy and Whitney's part in "Impossible" at this time of night. I knew Cole would want to see her when he left Matt but priding myself on being ahead of the game, I called Ava first and insisted she stay home until Saturday night.

"You two are still on to celebrate your six months right," Nugget asks.

Cole hiccups, the amount of liquor he's consumed has loosened his tongue. "I'm not holding my breath."

Oh the drunken anxieties of life. My cheeks pinch in amusement.

"Don't say that," Gail says.

I'd be as defensive as Gail under different circumstances. Let him suspect Ava. Let him spiral into an endless cloud of misery wondering if she'll ever love him back.

"It's true! Ava has been yanking me around for six months and I've let her," Cole says.

"Because you love her," she says.

Cole waits, thinking to himself. He's probably reminiscing about Ava's concerned and inquisitive deep brown eyes or her shy smile spreading wide unbeknownst to her. The thought mellows him. "I do love her."

The latest patron who enters the bar makes my blood cool and simmer simultaneously. I see her before she sees me. Her copper skin, naturally bouncy curls resting on her shoulders and penetrating hazel eyes lock onto mine as she struts toward me. Her beauty shines brighter under the cheap and dingy lights of the bar somehow. I will myself to breathe again. All these years later, my body still has a reaction to her. I pray I'm not as transparent as I feel. Rayvin slides in next to me instead of on the empty side of the booth.

I train my eyes not to stray from Cole. Rayvin slides her hand up my thigh to capture my attention. I stop her ascent pressing her hand into my leg, without letting go.

"Not what I called you for, Rayvin," I say.

"What matters is you called me, Casey. I know what we're doing tomorrow. Tonight we can spend together, right," she says. I don't respond. "You have to forgive me eventually."

She covers my hand with her other in a clasp, making my heart constrain as well. A long time ago, that is how she and I told each other 'I love you.' She knows exactly what she's doing, she always has.

"How can I forgive you?"

Rayvin smiles the smile I fell for when I was 15 years old. I believe in one great love and I wasted mine on a woman who gave her most intimate self to other people...for money, without protection.

And yet, when Rayvin gets out of the booth, I follow along like the puppy she trained. Tonight, isn't about regrets, nor making up for lost time. There will be time to talk, later.

"You don't have to leave so soon. You can stay a while longer," Rayvin says, rolling over to her side.

All I had left to put back on was my shoes. I turn to her before leaving her bedroom. "No."

Rayvin rises from the bed and lets the comforter fall from her chest. She doesn't need to tempt me with her full breasts my hands are twitching to get another hold of, her light eyes have always been what's held my attention. She's begging me to see her for who she was instead of what she's done. I concede. My heart brings me forward to comply.

"Does this mean you forgive me," she asks, removing my jacket from my shoulders as I join her back in bed.

I trail my lips up her arm. "Rayvin, I love you. And since you're here, back in my life..." The sudden optimism has me admitting, "I want you to stay."

She pulls me into her chest. "I'm not going anywhere. I'm here for you."

"You promise?"

"I do," she says.

We're starting fresh. I don't need to harp on what all she's unsuccessfully promised me before.

"I'll let you know if and when I'll need you," I say.

"I love you Casey," she says, pressing her lips to the back of my neck.

This time tomorrow, Rayvin and I will be starting new and most importantly the life I've always wanted, though never had the opportunity to have, will be mine.

CHAPTER 36
Ava

I spent the remainder of the week in and out of a variety of stores to shop for me and Cole's six month anniversary date. There were clothes I liked on the mannequin, not one me. Clothes I can't afford. And clothes in every size except my own. The mystery of a woman's body shape and wallet will never be equal.

Seven hours before Cole will be at my apartment to pick me up, I still have nothing to wear.

What does one even wear to a six month anniversary date to the diner you previously dine and dashed from?

And to think, a relationship like the one I've pretended to have with Cole is exactly what I've always wanted. I'm the fool who didn't know it required so much energy.

I've never had someone care about milestones. I need some serious and professional—of the fashion degree—help to be able to pull this off. I can't call Casey because he'll berate me for putting this much effort into it.

This sucks. Relationships suck. I suck! I'm hungry and tired and I fall face first into a stack of heavily perfumed sweaters.

"Ava?"

I remove my face from the proper pile of pullovers and see Gail. Great. Pretty, pretty Gail—with her flawless skin and perfect pixie cut, looking down on me at one of my lowest points. This day gets better and better. I don't know how Cole expects me to believe he and Gail are 'just friends.' Compared to Cole's kindness, and humility, how the hell did Gail choose Nugget's untamed red hair and idiot mouth spasms?

"Gail, hi!" I stand and check my surroundings hoping I didn't grab the attention of the entire store. It's just us. Now, how the hell did she find me here.

"I work here," she says, reading my mind. "At Express."

Wait, how did I get to Express? I can't afford Express.

"Can I help you find something," Gail asks.

I have no other chance of leaving the mall in an appropriate outfit without Gail's help. Somehow, she made an evening of games dress code appear effortless, cushy, with a dab of sexy.

"Please! Cole and I have our six month anniversary date and I don't know what to wear. I've been in and out of stores all week and I still have nothing to show for..." Gail bursts out in laughter. "...It...what...why are you laughing at me?"

"Ahh, no, I'm not. I'm sorry. You and Cole—two peas. He was here six months ago shopping for his first date outfit with you. Just as clueless. I saved him from buying a vest. Don't bother. I'll help you, too. Follow me," she says, walking deeper into the store.

"Uhh how about *you* follow *me* to Goodwill," I say.

"Trust me Ava," she says, offering her arm.

I hesitantly link us together, "Okay."

"Hello?"

Ugh, I scream in my head. Too tired to roll over to scream in my pillow. I've only been home from the mall for fifteen minutes. I dropped my bags at the door and went straight to bed to decompress.

I followed Gail through Express, then a few boutiques in the mall where she also had a discount, or friends with a discount. She found clothes to fit me plus looked good as I turned this way and that in the three way mirror. However, I wasn't pleased and comfortable until I was wearing a backless white tank top and black high waisted skinny jeans. Gail insisted on the black open toed wedges; which she explained gave my butt and legs the appropriate enhancement.

Now I only have three hours until Cole picks me up, meaning I barely have an hour to rest—considering I have to wash and straighten my hair. What the hell does Casey want?

He knocks outside my bedroom door, then enters and approaches the edge of my bed. "Your boyfriend—my brother, sure does have a way with words," Casey says.

"What?"

"I have his manuscript," he sings. I roll over and come up on my elbows to face Casey sitting atop my duvet. The setting sun gives me enough light to be able to read him. "Cole's written quite a story about a helpless boy falling in love with a helpless girl."

"Sounds familiar." I say, falling back into my pillow.

"Except this Aniya has a happily ever after with her oblivious beau, Elliot. Must be nice."

"Oh yea, Case. It's best to be completely out of touch with reality. What's the point in thinking men could build houses, stay faithful, and pledge themselves everlasting because you read it in a book?"

Our sarcasm stretches to annoyance.

His jaw ticks. "Hmm. You doing okay?"

My palms dig into my eyes. "I'm tired. I have less than three hours until my impending breakup and I've spent the majority of the day shopping—"

"You hate shopping." I'm so tired, I can't even feel a bit of warmth from Casey knowing me so well. He kisses my forehead. "I love you, Ava. Rest up before tonight. You don't have long. I want you to feel a little better—for yourself."

I drop back onto my pillow. I am no where in the mood for another bout of 20 questions I don't know the proper answers to. I get twenty minutes of sleep to bring out my best self...until I see Cole.

"See you soon, Casey," I yawn, as he leaves.

Hair, straightened.

Clothes, fit.

Shoes, will be my second greatest test of the night.

Mascara and eyeliner, waterproof.

This is as good as it's going to get. I rotate one last time in front of my full length mirror and leave my bedroom to meet Casey in the living room lounging on the couch.

"Yes queen," he greets.

I cover my nose with a snort and shake my head. Casey stands and comes over to me. He takes my hand and twirls me in a circle.

"I cannot tell you how much tonight means to me, Ava. Are you ready?"

Trying to keep my balance in the heels Gail suggested will be hard no matter how confident I feel. I nod in answer.

Casey looks me up and down again. "Damn girl. You look...mm."

Gail spent her shift picking out my outfit and accessories flawlessly as I followed her around. If this is Casey's reaction, I can't wait to see Cole's. Being dragged around the mall for four hours will have been worth it.

"Thanks," I say.

Casey reaches behind himself and holds a handgun in his palm. Upon seeing his offering, I take a step back.

"This is for you," he says. "Take it."

"Hell no."

"Get a grip, Ava. This is nothing you haven't handled before," Casey says. As Miss Green ingrained self defense among the girls, Casey's cowboy fantasies granted him a cathartic release at the shooting range. As roommates, he made sure I knew the ends and outs of gun safety, just in case. This is not the case.

"Not the point. What do I need a gun for?"

"Protection. Here."

Unfortunately...carefully I snatch the weapon from him. "This isn't necessary. Cole is not going to do anything to me," I say.

Casey grabs both of my arms and pulls me to meet him nose to nose. "Yes, he will. You are about to darken his rose colored glasses. You remember what I went through? Cole won't be far off."

Casey's smile widens and I tense. I don't want to be the reason Cole harms himself or harms me in retaliation. Who will be there for him like I was with Casey?

"Tuck it in the back," he says.

"Don't tell me what to do."

"Put the safety on firs—" he stops when I finish fastening the safety with a hard glare.

We face off with each other until I move the gun from my hands to the back of my jeans.

I hate Casey so much right now and I hate his parents even more for abandoning him which turned him into the person he is now. Most of all, I hate myself because I made Casey a promise.

I'm sure Cole has been dumped before. It's not possible I'd have the same influence Rayvin had on Casey. Cole has friends and a book to publish. If anything I've been holding him back for six months. When Cole loses me, I'm positive he won't lose sight of who he is supposed to be—an author—and who he is, a kind person.

By the end of the night, a weight will be lifted from both of our shoulders.

A knock sounds from the other side of the door.

"Oh my god." I check my watch, 7:45pm. "He's early."

Casey spins me back to face him as I go for the door. "Ava, look at me. Are you ready?"

I swallow down bile. Another knock. My senses are geared and heightened to Cole on the other side of the door. I want to get to him. Casey releases a long breath, then he places a kiss to my cheek and escapes to the back of my apartment.

When I answer the door Cole is dressed in his usual white button up with a black tie and black pants. Usual for him but damn sexy all the same. I drink him in from head to toe with my eyes, adding him to memory.

Thin yet solid frame. The hungry look in his eyes melting my insides.

"God, Ava. You're beautiful," Cole says.

"As are you."

His cheeks pinch at the compliment. "Are you ready to go?"

I take my time retrieving my purse and jacket because when I step out of the building, I'll be going from Cole's girlfriend to his worst nightmare.

When I meet him back at my front door he takes my hand and we head to our last supper.

Heather, the same waitress from six months ago—and owner, her updated nametag suggests, is waiting on us again. She doesn't seem like she's on guard and has yet to shackle our ankles to the table legs in case we try to run again. I'd say we're in the clear and free to enjoy our meals.

The soup of the day is French onion again and I begin stirring my ketchup covered French fries as Cole cringes. He shakes his head as I chew freely. I decide to hold conversation to keep me on task to set the proper temperature for the evening.

"Six months huh? Are you used to these kinds of relationships?"

"I'd say our relationship is something I'll never get used to, Ava. You're special," he says.

I've exploited and tricked Cole from day one, tonight will be anything but special. His sweet words are wasted. I eat another fry and soup combo and Cole shakes his head.

"Deja vu," he says.

"Mmm, then you have to try it again," I say. I bring a spoonful of broth covered potatoes across the table. "If we're doing things like we did six months ago...come on, you can't disturb the universe."

"That makes no sense." Still, he leans forward, taking the entire bite. Chew, swallow, water. Same routine, his face doesn't cringe this time; only his lips come together in a firm line.

"Ah, see. Not so bad this time," I say.

"Not...so bad," he agrees.

Cole and I continue our date and I notice him sneaking glances at other couples who are far more affectionate than we've ever been in public. I sense his energy levels depleting and make no comment.

"Ava, how would you feel about a trip?"

"Back to the Dunes," I hint.

"I knew you'd be a fan, but I was thinking somewhere inti-mate. For only us."

My mind flashes back to Enzo. The three days we spent together—'for only us.' And I never saw or heard from him again. Been there, done that, got rejected. I nod pretending to deliberate, knowing the answer I have to say.

"Is that a yes," Cole asks.

"Mmm. Don't you think that's kind of fast for us? I mean, we're still getting to know each other."

I see a twitch Cole masks with a one sided smile; like Casey. "Ava, we know each other fine. You're a beautiful, goal orient-ed romantic, with an aversion to chocolate and I love you."

Damn, he pays attention. He's seen my bookshelf and I told him about my dream of the suburbs; I'm stumped on how he knew I didn't like chocolate. There's no need to investigate now.

"Then why would you complicate things," I say.

"Me...complicate? You're complicated Ava!"

My hand comes to my chest, mocking anguish. My eyes water from poking my fork deep into my leg. Cole is getting angry which will leave him dumbfounded rather than trying to reconcile our faux pas when I finally get the words out to end it.

To push him further away from me, I pluck the dessert menu from between the ketchup and mustard to look over.

If I was looking up I'd bet I'd see steam coming out of his ears.

"Are you done," he asks.

"What about dessert?"

"Ava, we need to talk."

Yes! The three words a scheming girlfriend can't wait to hear. Cole will feel better if he breaks up with me. The dessert menu in front of my face keeps him at bay— "How about a banana Sunday to split?"

Cole throws enough cash on our table to cover our meals from tonight, six months ago, and a hefty tip.

"What're you doing," I ask.

He stands out of the booth with his hands tucked into his jeans.

"Let's go Ava."

I wave him away. "Go ahead. I'll meet you outside. I'll order a pie or something to go—"

Cole takes my arm and yanks me from the booth, pulling me through the diner toward the exit. Our dear Heather blocks our getaway with her arms crossed.

"I paid," Cole spits.

She looks over his shoulder where another waiter is counting the cash he left. He nods and Heather steps to the side to let us leave.

"I told you they'd remember us," I whisper. "Any chance y'all still have my coat?"

Cole whips harsh eyes to me and I wince. Out of the diner he drags me down the first alley lit by a flickering streetlight, pushing my back against the brick wall.

"Ahh!" *Oh hell no.* Now, I'm pissed. The way Cole grabbed and jerked me around was nothing like the boyfriend I've had the last six months and exactly like Casey. Cole doesn't have the clearance.

Casey has his reasons for being angry and lashing out, not Cole. Cole grew up with family and friends in the Carmel suburbs. He doesn't have the right to snatch and pull because his 'girlfriend' doesn't want to go on an intimate vacation. His hands are pinning my arms to the concrete wall. Without my jacket, the brick rubs my skin.

"Cole, you better let me go now," I say.

"No!"

"No?"

His eyes storm with a mixture of loathing and longing until he settles on indifference. Cole is the type of man to live by his woman, no matter how much it pains him. He releases me and starts pacing while mumbling to himself.

"What the hell is your problem," I ask.

Cole stops and something in my face makes him thaw his heightening emotions. When he takes a step toward me, I take one back.

"I'm sorry Ava."

His hand comes to cup my cheek as I turn my head. His hand rests on my shoulder, his thumb brushing my neck. I don't know how to deal with this version of Cole. I lived and grew up with Casey; we've put the time in to know each other and our responses. I don't know what Cole could do.

"I'm...I don't want to let you go. *You* keep pushing me away." His thumb moves up to stroke the side of my face, and I follow for him to hold my cheek in his palm. "Why?"

When I look at Cole my throat catches and my heart aches. This was not the revelation I was expecting upon hearing 'we need to talk.' Cole finds his valor and lets out a shallow breath.

"I know you're guarded, and for good reason. I need something from you...for you and me, right now."

"Like what," I rasp.

Cole moves closer to me, hooking his arm around my waist to press our hips together. I twist so his hand lands on my side and nowhere near the gun tucked in the back of my jeans. "I want to move forward with you and I can't do that by myself."

My lips search for words I can't say. "Cole..." Is all I can get out at the moment.

"Yes?"

"I uh...I..." Cole's lips find my right cheek. "Cole..." Then my left. "Um..."

He kisses each of my eyelids. His gentleness almost makes me come undone. "Yes?"

"I...can't..."

His lips freeze on my forehead. A moment passes before he brings us together, the sound of our breaths are heard right below the chaotic beating of my heart. Cole takes his time stepping away from me. Tears are wafting in his eyes. His large irises match the large lump in my throat.

"I want to be with you, Ava," he says.

How much pain will he put himself through? Let me go. "Why?"

Cole laughs to himself and wipes a hand down his face. "Why? Because—because Ava, when you're in love with someone there's no reason, only feelings! I fucking love you!"

His declaration bout sends me to my knees.

You love your car.

You love your job.

Love is materialistic and shallow.

Being *in* love? It's reckless and flawed and there's nothing to keep you from your someone. Cole's lack of sense has torpedoed him into impending misery. Idiot. How did he get through the last six months and find the nerve to fall *in* love with me? Cole doesn't even know me.

"You're in love with me," I ask.

Cole takes my hand and places it over his heart with a warm smile. He thinks he's won.

"I am more than in love with you, Ava," he says.

I close my eyes, when it's my ears I really want to block out. I wish Cole's confession was possible, him being able to fall in love with me. The real me. Instead he's a chess piece in Casey's game. We both are.

I step forward to Cole and kiss him gently on the lips. He lingers as I pull away. His eyes are still closed when I detach myself from his grasp to leave. He catches my elbow.

"I'm not going to wait forever," he says.

Case closed. Cole was never in love with me; and I'm thankful, he still has some sense left. Except his eyes tell me what he won't admit. He wants to beg me to stay and for a second I curse Casey for making me the bad guy. I know this feeling more than anyone.

"You'll wait. I know you will."

"This is it, isn't it," he asks.

Cole releases me and we stand off in the alley until he departs first, head hung low. What he doesn't know is he took a piece of me with him. The wall catches my back and I slide down the rugged slab, giving in to the pain radiating on my skin. I drop my face into my cupped hands. Rain begins to fall and I raise my head to the precipitation to cleanse my sins. My tears mixing with the water.

Thunder claps from above. Then an actual hand clap continues its rumble. Casey is coming from the back of the alley. I roll and wipe under my eyes as I stand.

"Even better than I could have predicted, A." He's vibrating in glee. "God, yes! He's broken. That sum bitch is fucking broken. You did it!"

I can't stay through his celebration when my heart is breaking. "So, we're done right," I ask and Casey stops. "I want my life back, Case."

"You don't have a life," he snaps. "And neither did I. Our parents never gave us a chance!"

"There's nothing else I can do. He's heartbroken, stranded and on his own."

"Good. Maybe he'll feel for a *moment* what I've felt all my life."

"Casey...Cole is without his family, job and soon his sanity the way I've been tugging him around. He's going to wait. He's going to go mad. He won't have anything to live for."

Casey's smile shifts to fifty shades of evil. "Exactly."

Woah, what? Casey starts past me but I step in front of him. "What? That is not apart of the plan!"

Casey pushes me to the side and I push him back. My reflexes have awoken to Casey's grand scheme. I plant my feet for his attack.

"Stop being so naive Ava. Where did you think my plan was leading up to? Did you think I put you through all of this to get Cole fired and broken up with?" He scoffs, looking down on me with complete malice. "I'll take it from here."

My knees relax. "Why didn't you tell me?"

"What the fuck did you think Ava?" His outburst is muted by the thunder.

"I didn't—I don't...No I didn't—" *Did I?*

"No, tell me what you thought I wanted from this."

"You wanted a family—"

"And they're dead. My entire family is dead," Casey says.

"Cole isn't."

His jaw works, I bout can hear his teeth scraping together. "He's dead to me."

"Casey, please. I didn't agree to this."

"You promised. To anything, remember," Casey says. "And this is only the beginning."

My bottom lip trembles. In my defense, I figured 'anything' entailed shaving off an eyebrow or peeing on his parents graves. In no way would I have agreed to destroy someone's mental well being so they'll...I hold my cramping stomach. My guilt weighs as heavy as a bowling ball.

Casey cannot be this vindictive to want to eliminate the only biological family he has left. Another clash of thunder brings me out of my head to...no one. Casey is gone.

What the hell have I done? Was I so childish and blind to what Casey always had planned? Casey tells me he's looking to harm Cole, enforce Cole to harm himself, and he thinks I'm going to go back to the apartment, pack and move back into our house?

What have I done?

I have to help him. Both of them. Reality television shows blend lost families all the time. I know Cole and Casey individually to bring them together to find forgiveness. To then move on as the best brothers. Casey's anger blurred my consciousness, I should have done this six months ago.

CHAPTER 37
Cole

My tears trailed behind me my entire walk home like bread-crumbs. How did tonight end with Ava and I breaking up? All I wanted to do was celebrate a milestone with the woman of my dreams. Now, I'm on the couch with four empty bottles of Stella at my feet. I haven't felt my emotions at once since my parents died: sorrow, confusion, deluded. Why did I give my entire self to Ava when she physically and emotionally told me over and over again she didn't feel the same way? In reality, this is my own doing. I played myself.

I still don't know what exactly it is that made me fall for Ava, I just know I was hooked from that first coffee stained day.

I don't know how to move on or how long this sorrow will last. Why even fight the suffering? It's better to love or some crap. I'll sit in it, live in it—I want to remember Ava.

"Cole!" Ava enters my apartment out of breath and without knocking, slamming the door behind her. Her previously straightened hair has coiled from the outside rain and drips along her face. She's fighting to catch her breath.

I sway when I stand, then widen my stance to level out. "Ava, what the—what are you doing here?"

She's back. Ava's come to get me back.

"Cole, are you drunk?" Her eyes begin to shine with tears, blaming herself for my current state.

Who doesn't begin to nurture their heartbreak with spirits of some kind? I thought I was going to be without her longer than an hour. I'm ashamed Ava seeing me the same way she's heard her mother acted.

I shrug. "I was sad. I'm sorry. I didn't expect you to see me like this." I've given my all to Ava, there's no use keeping the truth from her now.

"No Cole. You can't let someone like me have this sort of influence on you. Please. You can't," she pleads but all I notice is how beautiful she is no matter her streaked makeup, clumpy eyelashes, wet hair, and damp clothes.

"Someone like you? I love *you* Ava."

Her ankle shifts in her shoes as she makes her way to me to shake me by the shoulders. Doing the opposite to get me to focus, jumbling my brain. "Cole, listen. I am so sorry for all of this. I want to help and it will take a while for it all to make sense to you."

She's here. I commit her brown eyes and the reddened highlights of her skin to memory. If she thought she was leaving me again, I'm not letting her. Except why doesn't she look as relieved to claim me as hers? She looks scared.

"What are you talking about," I ask.

Ava moves her hands from my shoulders to my forearms, and her head lands on my chest. "I haven't been honest with you—about who I am. I'm sorry."

I lift her chin to look at me. "I love you Ava."

She rolls her eyes. "Shut up Cole and listen to me. I'm trying to talk to you. You and I weren't all real. Us meeting, you falling for me; it was planned by someone else."

Uhh... "Who?"

"Your brother," she says.

"Who?" *My brother?!* Is *she* drunk?

She takes a deep breath and pushes the fallen curls behind her ears—when she usually flips her hair out of her face. Ava isn't specific, she's erratic, hence the story she's concocted.

"Cole, listen! You do have a twin brother, his name is Casey. Casey Roberts. Your parents deceived you and abandoned Casey. He didn't die, he wasn't strangled. He's alive. Both of you have deep eyes, lanky build. He smokes cigarettes, the same cigarettes as you. While you've been loved and cared for all your life, Casey was my friend in the foster home. He grew up angry and he still is. He planned all this for you to have nothing...and no one."

"Including you?"

Ava nods, wiping heavy tears from her cheeks.

"Casey huh?" I laugh to myself, then laugh harder at the possibility of having an evil twin out to ruin my life. Ava came here to tell me a brother I never knew existed brought her in my life to take her away. Well— "He's on the right track."

I'm not sober enough for this conversation. I fall back into my couch with a wince. This couch is almost my age, any comfort has been worn out years ago.

Twin brother.

My parents are liars.

Casey's angry?

Okay well I'm pissed!

Ava's standing over me with imploring eyes. For what? This doesn't make any sense and is all giving a mid-day episode of Maury.

I allow credit for her being here, coming back for me. She could have let "Casey" enact the rest of his diabolical plan without a second glance. She comes to kneel in front of me, squeezing my hand in hers and holds my knuckles to her lips. My stomach warms.

"No, Cole. This isn't right." She cradles her cheek with our interconnected fingers. "I care about you. That's why I came back. I want to help the both of you."

This isn't possible. And the lack of possibility makes me want to laugh again. I hold it in and play along. Like from the moment we met when she tried to convince me she was a serial killer with eight kids. "How?"

"I need to find Casey. I came here first to make sure you were okay."

I kiss her hand. "I'm okay."

Ava's smile is small. "Stay here, please. Don't do anything or go anywhere until I'm back."

All I can compute is the beauty of Ava Hill. She lets go of me and pushes herself up from her knees to 'find Casey.' I open and close my palm to absorb the warmth she left.

"Oh my god—"

I look up at the sound of my door slamming shut again, and the tip of a switchblade pointed into Ava's throat by someone who looks exactly like me. I'm not looking in a mirror. This is...Casey. My brother. Ava was right. He's real. Alive. He's as tall, eyes are as brown and matching fade. He's me, except darker. His energy exudes malice. I actually have an evil twin.

I see mom's barely there eyebrows and our dad's strong hairline shaping my twin's face. Ava was right and we'll never know why because my parents—our parents are dead.

"Hello, brother," Casey snarls.

I'm walking a fine line of confusion—I have a twin brother? Intrigue—how do I have a twin brother? And nausea—I have a twin brother who wants to harm me and the woman I love.

I take my time getting to my feet from the couch. "C—Casey?"

He smirks. "Hmm. Isn't this an interesting turn of events Ava? We had a plan and you failed. You failed me, after you promised. I should have known I wouldn't have been able to trust you either," he says.

"Ah, Casey, listen to me." Ava struggles against his hold. I try to think an attack through. I need to protect Ava from my deranged twin brother.

"Shh, shh. Nothing to say now, A. It's brother bonding time," Casey says.

I find my voice. "No, Casey. Related? Yes. Brothers? No. You went and ruined my life, the life of someone you didn't care to know—went straight to scheming. Let it be over and remove your hands from Ava—now!"

"Or what?"

I take a step forward; Casey points the blade into Ava's throat. Her eyes widen and voice chokes, I stop my advance.

"What do you want," I ask.

"Casey, please. I'll do anything," Ava says, tears falling down her cheeks.

"I asked you to do one thing, Ava. And you failed."

"Ava," my voice breaks. My heart is breaking.

"I'm sorry Cole." She closes her eyes, giving in to the inevitable.

"God this is good. I knew this would be my favorite part," Casey says, throwing Ava into me.

I catch and steady her. My thumb runs from her neck, up to her cheek to make sure she's physically okay. Her eyes are pleading for forgiveness. Love can be myopic sometimes. Ava was dishonest and played me three ways to Sunday, yet I still feel love. I *only* feel love.

"Hello," Casey yells, waving his knife towards us.

Ava startles at the sound of his voice. I guide her behind me and connect our fingers.

"So, let me explain," Casey starts, talking with the sway of his hands. "Cole, our parents did have two boys born at 11:53pm—you and 11:58pm, me on February 23, 2001. And at 12:13am, February 24, our sister was born."

Casey points at Ava. The empty pack of Stella rolls in my stomach. I lock my knees to keep from heaving over. Ava gasps and tries to remove her hand from mine. I hold tight and her still.

"What the hell is wrong with you," I shout.

Casey shrugs. "Me? Oh, nothing. It's not like I was raised knowing the difference between right and wrong. You could not even imagine what Ava and I went through to survive, Cole. I got to play the game of life by myself, while Ava read her romance novels." He rolls his eyes and focuses on the woman at my side. "Are you listening Ava? Did you hear me? Our parents gave up the both of us so they could have Cole—love Cole. Cole was more important to them than us. Our parents loved him and hated us."

"That's not true," Ava and I yell.

None of this can be true. Ava's mom is dead. She's dead. Ava's mom is dead.

Right?

Casey is the only one who's done any research. The only plain truth before us is that Casey and I are brothers.

When it comes to Ava—the only mom she knew, or was told she knew, died. Case closed. She didn't need more answers.

"What about my last name," Ava rasps.

Casey's jaw clenches. "You were adopted. It didn't last long. James and Monica Hill—"

"My parents."

"Adoptive parents." he spits. "They thought a baby would fix their problems." He gives her a pointed glance of animosity. "You couldn't, Ava. And you were sent back to me after they destroyed each other. I never had the chance to go anywhere else, just so we're all on the same page. Ava, you meant nothing to our birth parents nor your adoptive parents."

"You are cruel, Casey," Ava's voice shakes.

"Cruel or right? We all weren't get put up for adoption and rejected from every family who ever visited? Right or wrong?"

Her hand goes limp in mine. Casey points his attention to me as if I have the answer to his years of rejection. I haven't a clue.

"This isn't fucking right," Ava screams. "Did you...Casey, did you know all this time?"

"No," he admits with a heavy swallow.

"And when you found out..."

"By then it didn't matter."

"Oh my God, Casey." Her face is etched in a multitude of distress. "Do you hear what you're saying? What you made me do?"

"You were *only* supposed to pretend! No one told you to open your legs—"

"Stop! Stop," I say. "What is this—what do you want?"

It's like I was in the audience of their one act play before Casey notices me. His sinister stare makes me wish I didn't say anything at all.

"Listen, Cole," he says. "You don't need to hurt your empty little head. *I* will get your life back together. *I* will get what you could never handle and more because *I* don't let my goals take a backseat because of a pretty face. I wouldn't have gotten this far otherwise." He laughs at his own sick and twisted logic. "Ava? I don't need you anymore. And no one will care to think twice about you. They never have. I've made sure of it."

Ava comes around me, wiping her cheeks. "What do you mean?"

He rubs his hand down his face. "I honestly didn't ever want it to have to come to this but you brought it upon yourself. You didn't have bad luck, A. You had me. I made sure your Dense Charmings lasted as long as I deemed necessary. Some of them tried to fight for you, though never hard enough. No one will miss you."

I can't imagine how Ava is taking this in right now. Her entire life has been a lie. Who she is? What she's lived—Er, maybe I do have a glimpse of what she's feeling.

"I will," I say.

"Ugh, bro are you fucking mental! She's our sister, fool! Do neither of you really know what I'm getting at?"

That sentence lands like a punch to the gut. "She's a person. I'm not going to let you diminish her any longer. She's...a person."

My eyes are leaking. I don't have the capacity to digest the amount of truth bombs exploding tonight because they're jumbled in my stomach and brain.

We wait. Casey drops his head into his palm and swings his knife between myself and Ava.

"You both will be dead by the end of the night. I'm tying up all my loose ends. From this night forward, I will be Cole Tace Roberts." *What?!* "And you Ava. You never had anything to live for. I've always wondered what kept you going all these years...doesn't matter now."

"Now, look here—"

"Shut up," Casey screams. "You don't know how long I've waited for this and you're ruining it with your holier than thou mindset. You're fucking done and—"

"Fuck you," Ava shouts.

Before I can comprehend what's happening, Ava releases my hand and is hurling herself across my apartment at Casey. He accepts his beating, punches to the chest and face. I head to separate them when he catches one of her arms, twists her to face me and plunges his knife into her back. Ava's eyes widen with a choked gasp.

"No!"

CHAPTER 38

Ava

Casey throws me away and I land on the ground. He lunges for Cole and I can't watch the person I trusted completely with my life attack his brother. My...?

Everything I knew about Casey and myself has been a lie. He was always in control, I never knew how much. I was as naive as Cole, oblivious to what Casey is truly capable of.

I wish I was dead. I'm forced to endure unimaginable pain while watching two hurt people, hurt each other. Two people I...

My body is split between mind numbing agony and finding a feasible way to help...someone.

Cole fends for himself as long as he can in his state until Casey gets on top of him and slams his head into the floor. Cole is out cold. Casey wipes under his bloody nose where Cole got a few good punches in before laying unconscious. He reaches for the knife he dropped and straddles Cole, bringing the knife high above his head and aiming down toward his brothers chest. There's no way Cole will survive this knife wound. Would Casey even stop after one strike? What karma have I encountered to have to watch this happen. I don't want Cole to die.

There's not much time or life I have left in me. I wasn't able to protect myself from Casey's wrath, there's time to protect Cole.

Wincing, I reach behind me until my hand comes around the barrel of the gun Casey gave me earlier tonight. The gun he gave me for protection from Cole.

"Casey stop!"

Either he doesn't hear me with the amount of adrenaline ringing through his ears or he's ignoring me. My hands are shaking as I aim for Casey's back. Through cloudy eyes, I don't wait or think about what I'm going to do because Cole doesn't have time.

When I pull the trigger the bullet slams into Casey's shoulder blade. He pauses, the knife slips from his hold and clatters to the ground. Blood seeps through his dark shirt, plastering the fabric to his back. He looks over the wound and the tears in his eyes, match mine.

Casey struggles to stand. He can't steady himself on two feet, falling on his elbow. With his good shoulder, he uses the one arm to crawl toward me. The persistence still in his eyes to see his plan through.

I don't lower the gun at his advance. He'll stop. He has to. "Casey, no. Enough. It's over, Casey. No! Casey!"

He collapses on top of me, the gun pressed between us. The weight of his body takes my breath away. His hands wrap around my neck and he presses with all the strength he has left. My cries struggle for release against his fingers.

I twist my arm under Casey. The gun digs into his stomach. I pull the trigger again and again until it's empty. When he's limp, I'm able to complete a full breath before screaming and crying in unison. I killed my best friend.

"Cole! Cole!" Tears blur my eyes and my screech comes out horse. "Cole, please—please!"

The front door kicks in. Two police officers, one extremely tall and the other extremely round, enter with their guns drawn, directed and scanning around the apartment. Cole unconscious, upturned furniture, and me beneath a lifeless body.

The taller officer puts the gun in his holster and carefully kneels to me. He flinches to protect his ears against my howls of misery and inner turmoil.

"Ma'am, please. Listen to me. You're going to be okay," he says. "Call the EMT's in! There's blood—a lot."

I don't let up. Such a broad word: okay. I've been abused and exploited and I'd always shrug with a 'yea, I'm okay.' Yet due to the amount I've seen and heard today, there's no possible way I will ever be okay again.

Officer Tall and Officer Round take their time assessing Casey on top of me and Cole in the corner. Tall and Round squat to get Casey off me.

"No—no!"

Tall stops and says, "What? What's wrong."

"Help Cole please. Please," I cry, looking across the apartment at Cole laid out on the floor.

Two paramedics enter behind Tall and Round. Tall and the first EMT are over me, while Round goes with the second attendant to check on Cole. I struggle for breath and my surroundings to rest when I feel the weight of Casey lift from me, his warm blood spilling on top of me. When they set his body to the side, I roll over to my elbow and retch over the floor. My sobs seize. My forehead falls on my arm. A few beats pass giving me the chance to catch my breath. I slowly raise my head and see Round is hovering over Cole with two fingers placed at the side of his neck.

"Is he—is Cole dead?"

Round turns to me, her face solemn. As she's finding her words, I try to find penance at the thought I've taken Cole from the world. The world is a dark place without him.

"No, he's not dead," she says.

"He's...not," I cry.

"He's not dead," she repeats.

I lay my back on the floor, tears leaking down the side of my face into my hair. The adrenaline from the past 30 minutes is seeping out of me.

Cole is alive. I did it. I saved him. My fresh tears are happy and I relish in my achievement that quickly morphs into searing pain. Then my world goes dark.

CHAPTER 39
Cole

Jostling transportation and a mounting headache is nauseating. With another jumble and jostle, my body aches from somewhere else. I try to ground myself and focus. Where is Ava? What happened to Casey?

My eyes flutter open to a sweaty man hovering over me.

"He's awake," he says to the front of the truck.

My eyes dart around, the ambulance and the severity of my possible fate engulfing me.

"Where's Ava," I wheeze.

The paramedic to my left removes the oxygen mask from my nose and puts his ear to my mouth. "What's that?"

Without oxygen, my breaths shorten. "Ava," I rasp.

He looks up and over me to whoever is at my head. "Was the woman's name Ava?"

"We don't know anything yet," the shadow above me says.

Our eyes lock again. "Do you know your name son?"

"Cole."

"What happened tonight Cole?"

"Evil twin," I pant between short breaths.

He frowns and shrugs his shoulders to whoever is at the wheel. "Lie still and take the oxygen Cole."

He situates the mask, my breaths come all the way in and out, and my eyes close while wondering when I'll see Ava again.

"Cole, my name is Dr. Wells."

A silver haired woman is standing at the end of my hospital bed with a chart in hand. If I didn't know any better, I'd think I'm face to face with my mom. They share the same features until you see the hard set of her mouth. My mom was hardly without a smile.

"Have you seen Ava," I ask. I laid still for hours enduring tests and probing to prove I am okay. A mild concussion is the least of my worries. Especially since the extensive questioning from the officers who were first on the scene let me know Casey didn't survive. I pray Ava hasn't suffered the same fate.

"Alright, you look good to go as long as you take things slow for about a week or so," she says, ignoring my question.

"Dr. Wells please." She slowly pulls her attention from the clipboard. "Do you know anything about Ava? She was stabbed tonight, she should have come in with me—before me. She was stabbed by my—" *Our?*

"You said that already."

I shut up and slam my head to the back pillow, unable to make sense of my life. Ava was stabbed and instead of getting her to the hospital, I was knocked unconscious. Too much time has passed and I still don't have an answer. And I still have too many questions.

Dr. Wells attaches my chart to the end of my bed. "I did see Ava."

I tilt forward, ready for more information. I've only seen doctors talk this slowly on television. I don't need a dramatic pause. I need answers. "And?"

"It's a waiting game as of now. Ava lost a large amount of blood before she got to us. We're watching over her. She came in unstable but made it through surgery without a fuss. There isn't much else we can do. Pray time is on her side."

My eyes leak. "When can I see her?"

Dr. Wells sees the emotion in my face and her facade of the professional doctor slips. She guides the wheelchair in the corner to my bedside. "I'll take you."

She transports me out of my room and to the elevator. We get off on the third floor. At this time of night—or early morning, the hallways are quiet despite the consistent beeping of various rhythms.

As Dr. Wells takes me farther down the dimly lit hallway I notice a theme with the passing patients: they're all pregnant—moaning through contractions or nibbling on ice chips. I pull on my brake and her knees slam into my back.

"Cole, what's wrong?"

"We're in—why are we in maternity?"

Dr. Wells comes to kneel in front of me. "Ava is in the maternity ward."

She lets me get there on my own. "Ava's pregnant," I ask.

Her brows come together. "You didn't know Ava could be pregnant?"

The last 26 years of life flash before my eyes. I've been to Europe twice. I'm getting my first novel published. Nugget and I already bought tickets for a five day all-inclusive Caribbean cruise for his golden birthday.

Now...I have a twin. Next year, I will be a father. Shit. Fuck! I remember the other bomb Casey launched and if Ava could be—

Wait. "What do you mean by *could* be pregnant? We're in the maternity ward. Ava either is or is not pregnant."

I'm not going to think back and wonder how Ava got pregnant. I only need to know if she currently is.

"If Ava is okay, the baby will be okay," Dr. Wells says.

I lift my hand from the brake and my face falls into my hands, stifling my tears. The loss of Ava could be two-fold. She's my family. Whether it's by blood or circumstance, we're linked.

I never thought about the possibility of a child, especially so soon. And especially with someone I don't truly know. Then the thought of my child being born from my sis—I can't stomach it. I can't go there yet.

Do I love Ava this much? I've loved her enough to wait and chase for six months and I know I'll be by her side until she's awake. Only to make sure she wakes.

Dr. Wells' hand lands on my shoulder in kind. I wipe the back of my hand across my wet face.

"Are you ready?"

Hell. No.

She takes it upon herself to unlock the brakes on my chair. I stare down the hall while my thoughts wild out. From this moment on, Ava and I will forever be invested in each other and I can't imagine how that looks.

Dr. Wells stops in the doorway. Ava is laying on her back with her eyes closed in her hospital bed. A lone light beams from above. Upon seeing her, I roll myself to her side as fast as I can and take her hand in mine.

I'm crying again. She's as cold and still as a corpse dressed in the same flimsy gown matching my own. My only guarantee of life is the rhythmic beeps keeping track of her steady heartbeats.

"What's her diagnosis," I ask.

"Like I said, we're waiting to see how...and if her body will pull through. A stab wound coupled with tonight's ordeal is a lot to wake up from. Her body could be protecting her from herself," Dr. Wells says.

"What do I—what am I supposed to do?"

I'm talking to no one, but Dr. Wells answers, "You can go now or stay?"

I snap to her. "What? Go now or stay."

"Leave now, Cole. Or stay," she repeats. I heard what she said the first time. I was giving her the chance to change what she said. Leave or stay? It's not that easy. Nothing with Ava ever has been. And now...

"I have seen a number of men debate with themselves about whether they should be a husband or father—"

Husband? This woman knows nothing about the last ten hours of my life. I keep quiet when she raises her hand to avoid me cutting her off and she continues. "You've been sheltered in the life you've lived prior on your own terms. Then, you met a girl and fell in love. You tell her how much she means to you and you'll do anything for her. And now you're here talking to yourself about what *you're* going to do?

"There is no *you* anymore. If you miss who you were before Ava instead of who you've been with her, leave now. If Ava wakes, a nurse will let her know her options. Otherwise, you stay and get ready for your pending future. Understand?"

I understand Ava has coerced me for months. How could I trust her? What possible future is there for us? I know what I have to do only in regards to the last ten hours of my life.

I'll leave Ava right now and never look back to what my life could've been before I was ready. Before I knew the truth.

Then I'll have the chance to take my time with someone else. Do my own research. We'll learn to love and grow with each other as a team. I'll never be in a half-assed situation again. I'll never be caught off guard into dating...

I find all my strength to stand head to head with Dr. Wells.

"You're leaving," she asks.

I start to make my way out of the room without comment. "Cole!"

"What?!" She gave me a decision to make and I need to make it now before another truth slips that no amount of therapy can see me through. "What is it?"

"You have to let Ava go."

"Yea, I'm leaving," I say.

"Cole..." I follow her pointed glance to my hand wrapped around Ava's. "You have to let her go."

I'm fighting against my heart and sense. I need time. I slope back down in the wheelchair. Defeated. Derailed.

Dr. Wells puts Ava's bed remote in my hand. "Press the top button for assistance. A nurse will come round hourly. Do you need anything before I go?"

I gasp. Ava's hand came around mine, she knows I'm here. I kiss each of her knuckles, communicating through my lips. *I'm here. I love—*

Fuck. I can't keep this war in my brain and heart.

"I'll leave you two," Dr. Wells says.

"Dr. Wells," I stop her. "What about the baby?"

"We need Ava's consent to perform more tests."

Damnit. Damnit. I open Ava's hand to rest her palm on my cheek. I may have to wait to be a parent, I'm not waiting any longer to know whether Ava and I can truly be together—are allowed to be together.

"Please. Please grant me this one request and then I'll be here. I'll wait forever if I have to, as long as I have one answer." *Are Ava and I related?* I don't let her know the favor would be against her oath. I need this.

"Okay," she promises.

I swallow my begging and bring Ava's hand to cradle my cheek. Okay.

CHAPTER 40
Ava

"Ava! Ava!"

I have to keep running faster than him. If he catches me, he'll attack. I'm running through darkness and fog. I can't stop. I push myself harder and farther so I can finally escape him.

His breath is on my neck as his footsteps catch up to me. I turn around without slowing down. No one is behind me. I smile triumphant. I did it. I'm free.

"Omph." My cheek smacks a wall. Not a wall, his chest.

"Ava." He's caught me in his arms. "You're not going any-where," he says.

I struggle. "Let me go—let go of me!"

"No, no. Ava, no!"

His warm hands hold my face and before I know it his lips are on mine. His kiss is hard until I melt under his passionate lips. I stop fighting his hold. I look up to him and then cry into his chest. He holds me as I wail and wail.

"Please, let me go," I say.

"I won't do that," he says.

"Why not?"

"Because I love you Ava."

I get that. I know being in love. It's all I ever wished for. Being in love doesn't make up for lies and betrayal. He needs to leave me or let me leave him. There is nothing either of us can do to be able to thrive with each other.

"You want me to say it again? I love you Ava. I love you Ava. I. Love. You. Please. Believe me."

I can't. I try and fail to push away from him.

"Tell me you love me," he says. "Say it."

I do love him and he loves me because I've meticulously shown him pieces of me. Once he gets the whole picture, he'll leave.

"No, Cole."

When I feel his grip slacken, I don't hesitate another moment to leave without looking back.

CHAPTER 41
Cole

Ava's been unconscious for the past three days. I've waited for a flutter of an eyelid or a pinky twitch but there hasn't been another reassurance of life since she squeezed my hand. Dr. Wells assures me Ava is fine and we're only waiting for her to come to. I am not fine with waiting to see if she will wake up after surgery. I need her to be alive.

Ava pushed through losing blood and consciousness to save my life. I've never loved her more than the day when our lives were threatened and turned upside down, because everything became clear.

All I've been able to do is pace her room and hover over nurses when they come in to check on her and—

"Cole..." she rasps.

Upon hearing the sound of her voice, I'm at her side in an instant, kneeling at her bed. Ava's eyes immediately flood with tears. She's awake. Alive, the harsh fluorescents doing her zero favors. Her color is drained, with sunken eyes and chapped lips.

"What happened," her voice scratches.

I kiss each finger then hold her palm against my face. She's weak, but I feel her try to pull away from me. "You are an incredibly brave woman, Ava. You saved my life."

Her throat works up and down without swallowing. I pour her a paper cup of water from her side table and put the rim to her mouth. She chugs it down to its base. "What has happened," she asks. Her voice growing stronger.

Thinking over the last three days, my mouth goes dry and the cup crumples in my fist. I struggle to swallow and update her on what she's missed.

"After you uhm...When Casey—"

"After the police stormed in," she says.

"We were brought to the hospital. I only ended up with a large bump on the back of my head and a migraine. You, on the other hand, have been out of commission since then because of..."

She turns away with a shudder at my recollection. The both of us will be haunted by Casey for the rest of our lives. "How long?"

I clear my throat. "Three days."

Her wet eyes blink at the ceiling.

"What about Casey," Ava asks.

"I wasn't allowed to see him. I was only told he didn't make it. He's dead. I'm sorry Ava."

I am sorry. For *her*. She's spent her entire life with a sociopath. Casey's demise doesn't affect me in the slightest.

"Casey's gone," she asks.

I nod. "I know you and Casey shared a history with each other. I know what he meant to you—"

"No," she says. "I...I never knew him to be against me. I thought he was protecting me...we were protecting each other."

A tear escapes and before I can wipe her cheek, Ava takes her hand from mine and does it herself. I want to take care of her except the last man who did looks exactly like me and landed her in the hospital where she laid unconscious for three days. Convincing Ava to love me now will be much harder than it was six months ago. It's the hand I've been dealt and there is no way I'm leaving her.

"I have something to show you," I say.

From Ava's bedside table I pick up the manila envelope and set it on Ava's lap. I hesitantly make my way to the edge of her hospital bed. I've been waiting three endless days to give Ava some sort of assurance for the future—our future. And it begins with what's inside.

Ava opens the folder and flippantly goes through the pages. "What is this?"

"A secret we have to take to the grave. Thanks to our doctor, these are three sets of blood tests from three different hospitals stating you and I are not related. Casey is my brother and there was another girl, Avalana..."

Ava closes the folder on her lap. "Avala...Ava could be short for Avalana. And my last name was Roberts once."

"You are Ava Hill." Just because Ava was born Roberts, she grew into Ava Marie Hill—ambitious, optimistic, loyal. "Blood doesn't lie. Three hospitals can't lie."

She looks at the inside of her elbow where a band-aid is stuck to her skin and she releases a relaxing breath.

Clearing my throat, I continue, "Avalana was only days away from adoption. She was 13—"

"13?"

"Yes."

"Lucky."

"She's dead, Ava," I say.

"What?"

While Ava's been fighting for her life, I was getting the facts Casey didn't look into. It was lazy of him to find out about three children and assume his closest friend with our sister's birthday was the same person without confirmation.

"A few days before Avalana's adoption was finalized there was a huge fight. A sort of ritual among the other foster kids in that home...if you get adopted over 12, your parting gift is a jumping. And uh, my sister didn't survive. She didn't make it to her family, she didn't even make it through the night."

Avalana's story is tremendously heartbreaking. I've mourned her while praying for Ava to come back to me. I never knew life could be so complicated. Fragile. My parents did a damn good job to shelter me from who they really were. All I ever wanted was siblings and I could have had two. What went wrong?

"No one ever wanted Casey. No one at all," Ava says into her lap.

"Ava, do not feel bad for that psycho, he—"

"Cole." I flinch at Ava's glare and shut my mouth. "You don't get it. All Casey ever wanted was a family. People go out of their way to prove they aren't normal and that's all we—he wanted to be normal.

"We wanted to race our siblings downstairs to the Christmas tree, or to Dad coming from work. Simple things." She wipes under both eyes threatening to overflow. "Your parents kept you. Avalana was so close to a family of her own, and Casey...Casey and I never—"

"I'm sorry Ava."

Of course I didn't think about how relaying the news to Ava would open old wounds. Her stream of tears match my own.

Ava's crying for Casey and the childhood neither of them got to have, which turned each of them callous and critical.

And I am crying for the siblings I never got the chance to grow up with and their unfortunate demise. Life isn't fair nor black and white.

"What does this mean, Cole? How did this happen? Your parents..." Her breaths are coming too fast. "Your...parents..."

"I don't know, Ava. I'm sorry. I wish I did."

"These are your parents, Cole! How have they...used all these people and now they're—"

"Dead," I say to her lap.

"They left...they left us in their wake to deal with this. How do we deal with this?"

With Ava in front of me, her nose running and tearful eyes; I still can't deny my feelings for her. And thankfully, I don't have to.

I want Ava to finally be honest with me, no matter how much we have to cry with each other to get there.

"Ava, was any of it real?"

She drops her hands from her eyes with a sniff. "What do you mean?"

I palm the top of my fade to buy myself time and courage. "I know what happened between us started as a master plan. We still have the opportunity for a different ending if you want one. Did I fall in love with *you*? Was the hijinks, stories, moments we shared together what you gave to me or were you only following Casey's script?"

"Cole—" She avoids my eyes to slip her mask back on.

She doesn't need to hide from me anymore. "Ava, you fasci-nated me from our very first day."

She hides her face in her hands. "Cole, I was conning you from our very first day. And I know I shouldn't have. I also know I shouldn't have agreed to Casey's plan but Cole you have to consider—"

"Do you read romantic novels, hoping for romance for yourself?"

Her eyes widen and lips open and close like a fish in water. "Cole, I—"

"And do you have a St. Bernard named Henry?"

Her fight leaves at the mention of her dog. Her true trusted companion. "Yes."

My heavy exhale is cut short by a great smile. Ava is exactly the woman I've fallen for. I was horrified at the thought of her being a robot of Casey's making. Without a brain of her own. A goal-oriented-romance-bookworm would only appeal to me.

The edge of my eyes prick with joy. "That's good news."

Ava stiffens. "There's more bad news?"

"I have great news, Ava." She lets me attach our hands. "I love you Ava. If I have to, I'll spend the rest of my life convincing you..." I move our joined hands to our future—her stomach. "The both of you."

"Both?"

"Ava, you're pregnant. You're pregnant and we're going to have a baby."

"We're...? No, we can't."

Damn. I always felt I was 'her body, her choice' except I don't want this family taken away from me. "What?"

"We cannot have a baby, Cole. I'm broke. Homeless—"

"We can get married," I blurt.

"What are you—This isn't happening. This can't be happening. We just found out...er, we don't even..." Her breaths shorten. A burst of perspiration peppers her forehead and upper lip. My knuckles crush together against her force. "No...No, I can't—" The machine bursts into a variety of sounds to alert the nurses station. They burst in and move me away.

"Ava? No." I try to fight my way back to her side.

The nurses are speaking to each other in a science I've never learned while they surround her.

"What is happening," I say, peeking over the nurses. "She was fine. She woke up."

One of the nurses takes me by the arm and walks me out of the room. "Let us find out," he says, closing the door in my face. I pace again until my stomach turns over on itself and I slide down the wall to wait outside her room on the floor.

Her door flings open, the same nurse who guided me out shuffles to the nurses station. He picks up the phone, says more rushed words that go right over my head, hangs up and goes to wait by the elevator.

Dr. Wells comes out, getting the recap of what I have yet to be clued in on.

Following Dr. Wells' tongue lashing and threatening her medical license, she's been my confidant, and I wouldn't trust anyone else with Ava. She gives me a small nod before entering Ava's room, the door closing behind her, shutting me out again.

Time stands still until the nurses and Dr. Wells exit one after the other. She squats down to me.

"Ava is fine," she says.

A small weight is lifted from my heart. "What happened?"

"Panic attack. Mild. We gave her a sedative to stabilize her heart rate."

I snap my head up. "Can you not do that again. A sedative. She doesn't...she could be likely to..." How do I say this?

"I get it. I'll make a note," she says.

"Thank you."

"I'm guessing you told her about the pregnancy?"

"Yes. I did...and I told her Casey is gone, how we're not siblings...I thought that'd make her feel better," I ramble.

"Cole, Ava has been through a lot and I don't mean in the last 72 hours. You'll have to give her time," Dr. Wells says.

I nod. I know. Time is all I've ever given Ava. Has it been worth it?

Dr. Wells offers her hand and helps me to my feet. We shake hands and she holds the door open for me to enter Ava's room and resume my place back at her side. My lips land on her forehead.

"I'm waiting for you Ava. Forever. I love you." I place my hand on her stomach again. Unsure what she'll decide, I have to say this at least once, "I love you both."

Chapter 42
Ava

I've been in and out of enough hospitals to know I haven't been subjected to any pain killers because pain is radiating throughout my entire body. Cole must have remembered when I told him about the reasons behind meeting with Blaine. I mentally thank him as my eyes flutter open and I look around the room: cheap lighting, rushed voiced seeping in from the door being left cracked open, and not another person around. Cole isn't here. My dreams weren't too high, I knew he'd leave me sooner or later.

I wince as I scoot up the bed. My limited strength fails and I use the bed remote instead. Tucked between the mattress and the rail is the manila envelope I opened from Cole before. I wait a beat before psyching myself up to a world of unknowns. Will he ever know the full truth—will I?

Except inside is not the documents from the three hospitals he mentioned. It's a 4x6 size printed picture of Cole, Henry and I.

Cole visited me at work plenty of times. So many times, he became used to being around Henry's size and energy. When Greg wasn't being a mansplaining dipshit, my annoying co-worker happened to snap a candid photo of Henry, Cole and myself. Cole's legs hanging from my desktop smiling down at me, I'm smiling up at him from my chair and Henry looks at us both with his tongue hanging out the side of his mouth. We're all smiling. We're all happy.

I pick up the photo and notice handwriting bleeding through the other side. When I turn it over, Cole's message brings, a lump to my throat.

Ava

you are <u>more</u> than enough to be cherished and loved.
forever, Cole

I reread his words until I commit what he's said and his light penmanship to memory.

"More than enough," I repeat to myself, a tear escaping and landing on the photo.

There's a knock on my door. I tuck the photo under my gown, then wet my finger with my tongue to smooth out my eyebrows and wipe underneath my eyes, hoping Cole has come back. Without knowing what my hair looks like, I try to calm fly aways by raking my fingernails as far as my untamed coils will allow. They glide a quarter of the way through before snagging. I give up and answer. "Yes."

A gray haired woman in a lab coat enters and my face falls.

"Good afternoon, Ava. My name is Dr. Wells. I've been in charge of bringing you back to life...so to speak."

I laugh softly, as her lips remain in a firm line. "Nice to meet you."

She takes the chart clipped to the end of my bed and looks it over, determined yet distant. She looks up to me with a cool smile.

"Well, I'm sure you're ready to get out of here and as far as I can tell, you're fit to go home. As long as you remember you're still recovering from surgery, so limited activity and drink plenty fluids. We can get you out of here in a couple of hours. The OB/GYN needs to check the health of your baby. They'll also be able to answer any questions you may have," she says.

"You're not an OB?"

"No, I'm general—"

"Which means you're specialized in the whole lot."

Dr. Wells drops the clipboard to her lap. "Ok. Do you have a question?"

"Uh, yea. Could you please specifically concentrate on me? You've been here with Cole. Cole had you look over me the last four days, you know me. You know us. Please?"

Dr. Wells face relaxes into compassion despite herself. She lets out a long breath and sets my chart at my feet. Inwardly,

I'm leaping for joy when she leaves and returns with an ultrasound machine to place at my bedside.

I lean back and take deep breaths. My heart is racing, beating against my ribs; I'm about to see my baby for the first time. Now that I'm awake, what I said to Cole is like a distant dream. We both said things in the heat of the moment. I wonder what he remembers and what he meant.

Dr. Wells snaps latex gloves on her hands and stands above me, waiting. I fidget not knowing what the hold up is.

"Leave the blanket over your legs and lift your gown above your belly button," Dr. Wells instructs.

I oblige silently, trying my darnedest to find my resting heart rate. I don't want to crash out again. I'm still while my nerves and sense ping off each other.

"This gel helps for a visual and it'll be cold." She doesn't give me enough mental time to prepare and I flinch when the gel lands on my abdomen. "I'm going to use this wand to spread the gel and then your baby will appear on the screen. Any idea how far along you are?"

"Not...really," I admit, apologetic. Cole and I should have taken better caution but too late to go back now.

"Okay." We both turn to the black screen.

Dr. Wells places the wand on my lower abdomen and the screen illuminates in black and white. She searches then lands on a disproportionate bean.

"Ah. There it is..."

"I don't hear anything."

"The heartbeat will be audible in about three more weeks. I'd say you're around 6-8 weeks pregnant. It's also too soon to tell the sex." Oh my god. It's a pea. A sweet pea. I've done something I can't take back with someone who isn't here. Where is Cole? "Not much to see or disclose now. On your follow up appointment Dr. Maddox may be able to show you their webbed fingers."

I scrunch my face and Dr. Wells side eyes me with a smile.

"Who is Dr. Maddox?"

"Our OB—the best OB. I've been updating them on your recovery so they'll be informed when you meet." I open my mouth to protest but Dr. Wells continues. "Dr. Maddox is prone to dysfunctional stories. You and Cole are perfect. And will be properly taken care of. Congratulations, Ava."

She winks and uses a damp towel to remove the excess lubricant, then moves my gown back down my body.

"Thank you," I say.

"Are you in any pain?"

"Kinda sore."

"You haven't been active for awhile. Your muscles will take time to recoup. I recommend two aspirins, twice a day. Can you handle that?"

Dr. Wells regards me with an intense glare. Geez Cole, talk much? I nod and she starts out of my room.

"Is Cole here...or around...anywhere," I ask.

"I'm sorry, no."

The back of my nose stings. "Ok."

"Cole has been by your side the entire time, Ava. I have no quandary he'll make a great father," she says.

A great father. Not a great partner.

I am pregnant with Cole's child and Casey's niece or nephew. When did my life get this complicated? Dr. Wells is sure of Cole's parenting role. What about me and Cole? How far can we really go with each other? Our baby will keep us together now. What happens when we finish decorating their college dorm and they're ushering us out to begin their own life? Will Cole and I then go our separate ways? Are we still temporary?

Dr. Wells leaves my room and I clutch my chest where my new favorite picture is. The time has come to checkout of the hospital and into the inevitable.

CHAPTER 43
Ava

If I've learned anything in the last six months, it's to do your own research before making decisions that could affect your life and the lives of others. The first two days upon leaving the hospital, I was neck deep in intensive research to find the one person I needed to see first.

I can tell Avalana Carter, Cole and Casey's younger sister—their triplet, was going to be well taken care of by the way her parents commemorated her memory. I've been posted across from her crypt for hours and it's as beautiful as I believe she was. She's plated around white marble inside of the mausoleum at Crown Hill. She'll be protected from various weather conditions and time.

Avalana Shawn Carter born February 24, 2001, died March 2, 2014. Below her life span, her adoptive parents inscribed 'beloved daughter.' Avalana, one of two abandoned children of Toni and Shawn Roberts was a 'beloved daughter.' It's a beautiful sentiment. She was loved. No matter how brief.

Casey's headstone will only have his name and life span. He wasn't a husband or father. He was barely a friend. He had dreams that failed in comparison to his conceit. Casey Roberts lives on only as a haunting nightmare to those he affected with his antipathy.

The wind picks up and the rain begins smacking the building. My words stumble out.

"You don't know me. And...I wish I could have gotten the chance to know you. I'm Ava—just Ava. Avalana is a beautiful name. I wish we didn't have to meet like this. I'm sorry for your parents loss. I wish Casey would have gotten the chance to save you the way he was able to...save me."

My throat threatens to close but I drudge through. "All things considered...he did get me through the last 26 years with barely a scratch—if we ignore the last two weeks. Casey's gone now and I'm going to start taking care of myself—by myself.

"He was my best friend before he found out about you and Cole. I wanted so bad to help him. I couldn't help Casey *and* fall for Cole. I love Cole, I do. And I promise to be good to him." I stand and pull out the first sonogram Dr. Wells gave me of my sweet pea, my tears falling down my cheeks.

"I want to leave this with you. Please look over Cole, myself and your niece or nephew. Goodbye, Avalana."

I sit in my tears before rising to stick the sonogram in the corner of her frame and add six white roses to the side vase.

The mausoleum doors open and slam shut due to the wind bringing in scattered debris. I look to the entrance where the shadow of a man is standing stock still.

"Why are you here," he asks.

I swallow my hurried breaths and squint for a better look at the stranger who comes out of the shadows, making his way toward me. He's haggard and hunched except I can't smell the fumes that plagued my nostrils the first time we met.

"George?"

"Girl," he says.

I roll my eyes. "You know my name is Ava."

"You're Cole's girlfriend."

Okay so he will call me 'girl' and 'Cole's girlfriend' not my given name, got it. I wonder how long it took him to stop calling Cole 'boy.' Maybe I should buy him a sandwich.

"Yea," I say to him. "I think," I mutter to myself.

"What does that mean?"

"What are you doing here," I divert.

"I work here," he says. George nods to the headstone over my shoulder. "Who's that?"

"Long story." George waits. "She's like uhm...an angel."

"Is Cole okay?"

I swallow hard. "I believe so."

"You gonna be good to him," George says.

My eyes well and throat constricts. There's a nagging thought that even though Cole loves me, he could still leave.

"Cole is a good guy...one of the best," George continues. "Before I was working here among the dead, I watched upon the living. I noticed how people treated themselves and each other. Cole, he shines among the fog and chaos of the world."

I wipe away a tear. "I know."

"He's not immune to pain. Hell, no one is but he's one of those people people like us need to protect. You and I have lived in a dark world. We need Cole to shine."

"I...I, uh...I won't hurt Cole." I won't hurt Cole, *again*. George nods and turns down the hall.

I have the most important person growing inside me. I know I'd do absolutely anything for this child. I'll never leave. I'll always be there to support them. I'll protect and care, we need Cole to give them love. I want our child to glow as bright as Cole with love and true promises.

CHAPTER 44
Cole

"Bro, you could have died," Nugget yells, his face growing to match the shade of his hair. He's been hounding me ever since I got to his apartment. Being stuck to Ava's bedside, I've been ignoring my friends calls and messages, it's time to face the brute of their anger first thing in the morning. I haven't showered, Gail is still in her bonnet and Nugget has never been a morning person.

Nugget is furious—two fold, and Gail is simply scared. She hasn't said much because she's looking over my cuts and bruises, making sure I really am in one piece.

"Ava wasn't going to let me die," I say.

"You have got to be fucking—Cole, how could you possibly fucking think—"

"Nugget, please," Gail says, from the chair by the couch.

Nugget and I have always been thick as thieves. The years we spent growing up together made us more than friends, we're brothers. I've taken him for granted considering how unhinged my actual brother is—was. I despise having to defend my feelings for Ava but she is pregnant and I'm in love with her. Case closed.

"You talk some sense into him then," Nugget says. He huffs from the couch and stomps off toward the kitchen, I hang my head in my hands.

We have been talking in senseless circles about what if's for over an hour. The moral of the story is Ava did save my life. I can look past her lies and manipulation when she ultimately gave me an opportunity at life—a brand new life.

Even through the yelling and holding back of tears, there is still a mix of angst and relief radiating between Nugget and Gail. It breaks my heart to think about them mourning me if Casey set out what he wanted to accomplish. He didn't. I'm here.

Gail leans toward me, taking my hands in hers. I keep my head hung. "He wouldn't listen to Ava either." I come up puzzled. *Ava was here?* Gail nods. "She came to see us and apologize. Hoping we'd forgive her."

I perk up a bit. Is there a chance my best friends and girlfriend will get along? Gail shakes her head and my face falls.

"Ava, she...she went through a lot to destroy you Cole." Gail's cheeks catch her tears. "Even if she didn't know how far things would go—"

"She didn't know!"

Her lips form a hard line. "I know she loves you." Her confession on Ava's behalf brings me up short. Maybe it's women's intuition because Ava has never said such words to me. I start to come up in glee. "Is that enough," Gail continues and my joy sinks. "We get it, she didn't succeed but what if she did—what if Casey did? Have you thought about that?"

Casey doesn't matter anymore. I won't continue to give him a place in the new life Ava and I are headed toward.

"I think about how my child could have been raised by Casey with Ava still under his thumb," I say.

"So it's about the baby," she asks.

I nod. "If there is still a baby...I'm going to protect them both."

The corner of Gail's mouth twitches in a semblance of a smile and there's a peak in my sorrow. I'm officially in daddy and partner mode. I have a family to defend.

"Cole, Casey is gone. No one would be coming for them...or you."

"Gail...His memory remains for Ava and myself. It won't for our child. She will be safe and happy."

"She?"

I shake my head with a shrug. "I'm assuming." The thought sending a flutter in my belly.

Nugget returns with three open Stella's in hand and collapses on the couch.

"It's 7am," Gail says.

" Sue me. Are you dumping her or not," he asks, starting to pass around the bottles.

"No," Gail and I say.

Nugget pulls the Stella's back to his chest. "Get your own then."

Gail and I share a resigned smirk. My bottom lip trembling at having someone closer to seeing my view of things. Gail can help Nugget recognize why I'm doing what I'm doing. I mouth a 'thank you' to Gail and she places her hand on Nugget's knee. He chugs one beer and goes for the other, leaning his head back, a tear slipping down the side of his temple.

I put my hand on his other knee, patting him twice. "I'm okay, man. I promise."

My best friend pushes my hand off him. Gail takes my hand and reaches for Nuggets, fusing us together.

"Cole has responsibilities now and we're going to be there to help," she says.

Nugget belches in response.

CHAPTER 45

Ava

Upon leaving Avalana's grave, I went to see Nugget and Gail to explain. In reality, Nugget answered by screaming in my face for two hours. My sister-in-law was a much better listener. Now, I am spent. I wish I could go home and begin packing up my apartment and finding a new place to live. First, I have to see Cole. Before I begin my new life, I need to know if he'll come with me...us.

As I work up the nerve to knock on Cole's door, he opens it on his way out and stops upon seeing me. I don't know how I want to begin, and the words I do know aren't coming out. Cole is bruised and stitched shut and so is my mouth. I can't believe I had a hand in damaging someone so beautiful.

"Hi," he says. I nod. Cole opens the door wider. "Come in."

I take a step away. "If you're heading out, I can come back—"

"Ava, come in," he says.

My legs move before my mouth can chicken out. Cole shuts the door behind me and I break out in a cool sweat remembering the last time I was here. I try to steady my breaths, blinking past the memories: Casey's hand in making sure my dreams of falling in love would fail, the bullet hitting him in the back, me screaming for Casey to stop—that it's over. The chill rolling through me snaps me back to the present where I'm standing in the poor excuse someone did to clean the blood from Cole's aged linoleum. Mine. Casey's. His.

Cole makes his way around me, standing a few feet away. Even with the amount of remorse wafting through me, my body wants to close the gap between us. He's standing taller than I feel in gray sweatpants and plain blue T-shirt.

"Sorry about the mess, I haven't been home since—until today," he says.

"Cole, I am so sorry. About..." I gesture around his ruined home. If not only in setting, the constant reminder too.

Cole shrugs. *Shrugs?!* "It's replaceable."

I scrape my nails against my head as far as they are able to reach. My hair is still in the botched ponytail from a caring nurse or the caring man before me. "You...you can't forgive me." I gesture around his apartment: broken glass swept in a dustpan, upturned furniture, blood stained linoleum.

"I love you Ava. And I know we've had an unconventional start and middle..."

My tears unleash and my head pounds through my ears. I began falling for Cole when he believed in my dreams. I loved Cole when he let me know I wasn't a conquest, that I was a befitting companion. I don't want him to love me in spite of the last six months. I want him to love me because he's sure I love him. I haven't been honest with my feelings for Cole. Before, I was only a person used. Now I can be more—a mother and...

"Stop," I say.

"Stop what," he asks.

"Stop being so perfect. I need to prove myself—my love for you. Gail and Nugget need to believe it too, okay?"

Cole's eyes widen. I've said something wrong. He doesn't want me. He needs more time.

"You love me," he says.

What? I need Cole to yell at me, that's what I was prepared for. I knew I had to beg and wait for Cole to come back to me. He can love me all he wants while realizing the amount of danger I put him in.

"Cole, I almost got you killed—"

"You said you love me," he says, taking conscious steps toward me.

I let out a long breath. Cole won't listen and his proximity is threatening my resolve. His eyes are straightforward and his fingers are twitching to get a hold of me. If he's going to be delusional, I'm going to be grateful. I invoke he's not euphoric now to shun me later. I will myself to finally give my entire being over to Cole Tace Roberts. He'll take great care of me.

"I love you Cole. You are everything I could have ever imagined in a man...and in a father—"

I choke back sobs, unable to continue when Cole takes two large steps to look down on me and bring our mouths together. My tear-stained face cradled in his hands.

"Marry me," he says, breathing heavily.

My breaths and coherence are at odds on which one matters more. He remembered. "Wh—what?"

Cole's thumbs wipe beneath my eyes. "Ava, I know deep down a part of me has loved you since we dine and dashed, since the first time you left me outside of your building—leaving me wanting more. I loved you since our first kiss and especially our second kiss; and most importantly since you graced me with the chance to have a family again.

"We—you and I...we didn't have the upbringing we wanted but we can make sure she has it all." He places a hand on my stomach. "Starting now."

Her. "You think it's a girl?"

Cole smiles, his teeth shining bright in my eyes. He brings his other arm around my waist and my stomach flutters. I know it's too soon for the baby to kick. What I feel now is cherished. Finally.

"Marriage," I ask.

"A family! Me, you, baby girl, Henry..."

He didn't forget about Henry. Henry gets to come home.

"Will you marry me, Ava?"

I didn't fall for Cole, I slammed face first into a wave of ecstasy which swallowed me whole. I have no way out, but first—

I step out of his hold and his face falls.

"How did you know," I ask.

"Know what?"

I clear my throat and stay put, no matter my need to run full force into the future Cole is extending.

"How did you know I didn't feel I was enough...to be...in your note—"

"Loved? You're enough to be loved." I move my face to avoid looking him in the eye. When both of his hands cup my cheeks I become locked on him and his words. "Everyone wants to be loved Ava. Everyone. The only people who are crazy enough to reject it, must not believe they are good enough, smart enough, or beautiful enough. And you, baby...you are all of those things." He opens his arms. "Will you let me?"

I smile. "Yes."

Cole calls me forward with his hands and I jump into his arms. His hold comes around my back and I wince at the pressure. Cole pulls back immediately.

"Are you okay," he asks.

"I'm okay," I reply. It was something like a week ago when I thought to myself how I'd never be okay again when the paramedics arrived. Here I am today, okay.

I step back into his chest and rest my head on his heart. The heart that loves me.

I've spent my entire life with the wrong people and their unlimited amount of selfishness. My remaining days on this earth will be with the man I love, our baby, and Henry.

EPILOGUE
Cole

I've read the books, went to every lamaze class and even crashed a few 'mommy and me' clubs. I am ready. I have to be.

Neither Ava nor I have been around children—babies since we were children/babies. Ava has glowed and swelled the last seven and a half months beautifully. And coming up on 28 hours of labor my wife is using all her strength to bring our child into the world.

Her knotless braids are tied in a pineapple bun on the top of her head and I try to catch the few slipping out so they won't attach to her sweaty skin. I keep kissing her cheeks, nose, forehead in devotion and support. She prepared to perform the birth naturally. And then six hours of contractions later, she wanted an epidural. Unfortunately by then, it was too late. I can't imagine the pain she's going through.

"I love you so much Ava. You're doing great—"

The flare of her nostrils rise and fall. "Am I? AM I? Where. Is. He—AHHHH!"

As I've fallen for Ava more and more throughout our marriage: moving into my parents house, my book getting published and picked up for a series—Ava has endured mood swings and bouts of nausea with a low smile. I've been proven amazed by the wonders of her body that brought us to this moment.

Over a day of perspiring and months of wondering how her body will deviate next, there's finally an end to this trial. She's more than ready for our child to be born.

"Ava, come on—we're almost there."

Ava's sharp eyes snap open and to my face. "There is no we. Not right now Cole," she says through clenched teeth. "I. Got. This."

I nod. "You're right. You're right, baby."

Dr. Maddox, highly recommended by our friendly Dr. Wells, pokes their head up between Ava's legs, determined.

"Alright Ava, one more push and you're home free. Er, home free to the eternity of motherhood. One more push and you'll never have a moment to yourself again. It'll be diapers then puberty intertwined with never ending fear—"

I obnoxiously clear my throat. Highly recommended and unfunny. Ava stares them down.

"Right." Dr. Maddox gets back into position.

Ava is hanging on to the bedrails with all her might to keep from pushing and I bring my hand over one of hers.

"Ready, Ava," the doctor says. Ava groans twisting her head side to side. "Ava, now! Push!"

Ava rises with closed eyes to focus on pushing down, growling from the pit of her stomach as Dr. Maddox is counting down from ten, until we hear crying. Weeping coming from neither of us. Ava looks to me to confirm and I nod. She collapses back into the hospital bed to catch her breath.

"Yes! We got her," Dr. Maddox says.

I try to get a peek over Ava's knees. "Her? We have a girl?"

Ava and I were split on the sex of our baby. Not knowing and placing low bets kept our spirits high.

Dr. Maddox raises our daughter, squirming in their hands. She's covered in blood and vernix from the womb and screaming into the void.

"Cole?" The nurse offers me a pair of small and precise scissors to cut the umbilical cord. My hands are shaking up until I get to the cable attaching my wife and daughter. My hands are still and sure, cutting my baby girl free.

"Good job, Cole," Dr. Maddox says.

Dr. Maddox and their nurses take our daughter to the side to wipe her clean and administer the physical exam. I don't take my eyes off the nurses hunched shoulders until my baby's cries subside. Ava tugs my shirt and I come down to kiss her again. Once on the lips and then all over her face.

"You did it," I say.

"I love you," she responds.

Even though we have made a number of strides these past months: debating whether or not a flatbread is considered pizza, Nugget being able to make eye contact with Ava during our baby shower, and our long weekend babymoon in Cincinnati; I never take for granted her loving words towards me. I fuse our lips together, tears leaking from the corners of my eyes.

The sound of baby gurgles come up behind me, I turn to a nurse ready to hand over my child. Her tiny hands are crossed and framing her heart-shaped face. I choke back sobs when I notice my dad's broad nose above Ava's full lips. Then the eyes of my daughter, looking like mine, flutter open to take me in. I am my daughter's first viewing.

Parenting stereotypes say all newborns look alike but I know this child is mine and Ava's. I've also heard a parents love for their children can lift a car or rescue them from a burning building unscathed. I would kill for this little one in my arms.

"Cole."

A nurse pushes a chair up behind me and I give my legs a break, coming to Ava to introduce her to our daughter.

She gasps. "Oh my god, she's amazing."

From husband and wife to mommy and daddy. I never knew how soon those character labels would apply to me. I stand to place our child in Ava's arms. Looking over my two girls, tears spill down my face and land on Ava's cheek.

"Oh, baby," she says, reaching to wipe my cheek with the pad of her thumb.

"I'm...gah, I'm sorry. I haven't slept and I'm happy. So happy." I kiss my wife on the forehead. "You make me so happy Ava. How did I get so lucky?"

"I ask myself the same thing. I love you Cole." Ava scoots to the left of her bed, allowing me space with my family. I wrap my arm around Ava's shoulders and place my hand on my daughters pink bonnet covered head. I could live in this moment forever.

Ava rests her head in the crook of my neck and yawns at the exact time as the bundle in her arms. Ava perks up.

"Did you see that? We yawned!"

A nurse comes to the end of the bed with a clipboard tucked under her arm. "You two will want to capture this."

My lips touch Ava's forehead again before I reach into the pocket of my joggers and hand my iPhone to her. She swipes to the left to open the camera and brings it up to put my family into focus and snap the occasion.

"Perfect," she says.

Dr. Maddox peeps over the nurses shoulder. "Agreed," they say. "Ava, in about five minutes we'll take you to recovery okay?"

Ava's eyelids are drooping when she nods. Dr. Maddox leaves our room and I retrieve my phone from the nurse.

I check the photo and my chin quivers. Ava's smile barely lifts her cheeks, tired and endlessly beautiful; our daughter in her arms, her deep brown eyes wide and searching. And then there's me, holding both my girls in my arms, my smile the widest it has ever been. Tired, wide eyes and flushed cheeks; my picture perfect family.

"Mr. and Mrs. Roberts, we need your signature for the birth certificate," the nurse says.

Ava and I both sign upon the dotted line to legally claim our daughter as our own.

"Do we have a name," she asks.

Ava turns to me with eyes as wide as a boulder. "We never talked about it. We wanted ten fingers and ten toes. And I was sure I was having a boy. I didn't think of girl names."

The nurse offers an understanding nod. "We can always fill in that blank later. Are you ready to get some rest Momma?"

Mine and Ava's eyes water. The miracle of life is a whirlpool of emotions, most specifically, tears. Tears of happiness, tiredness, love. I get up out of Ava's bed and hold out my arms.

"It's okay Ava, I'll look after her," I say. She presses her chapped lips against our daughters forehead, cheeks, chin and nose; laughing to herself when she hands the baby over.

The nurse unlocks Ava's bed wheels and rolls her out of the delivery room. Swaying with my daughter in my arms, I add a little bounce and a soft hum. I peek under her pink beanie to see a head full of dark brown straight hair. I'm already wrapped around this little girls finger, who has taken on my characteristics to fit her perfectly.

When my knees start to get weak, our nurse comes back in. "Daddy's need rest too," she says.

Daddy. The waterworks return.

The nurse ushers a clear bassinet in front of me and I carefully place our daughter inside, covering her with the blanket Ava taught herself to crotchet. They go off to the nursery and I go find Ava's room for recovery.

Ava grew up in a twin bed. I've always had a queen. She's had little space of her own and still hasn't gotten used to absorbing the new space allotted to her.

At six months pregnant, Ava welcomed my invitation to move into my parent's three bedroom house with me. She lasted three weeks living back in the house she shared with Casey, then agreed to move into my studio to reduce the number of panic attacks she was having due to what she knew before and what we know now. The only thing she brought were some clothes, all of her books, and Henry.

Many nights I watched her sprawl in my open bed to end up curled along the edge. She's prone to dancing throughout the kitchen with no music playing. And somehow she still puts herself in the corner before too long.

Like at home, she's laying on her side along the edge of the bed. I climb into the empty space next to Ava, she turns into me and places her head on my chest. Bliss.

Cole

There are loud heels clacking down the hallway past exhausted new mom's rooms. Her height and stature combined with her bronze toned skin is the envy of every new mom who won't see their pre-baby body for awhile. Her mystery exudes the dark and sinister qualities of a raven.

She lingers outside of the maternity ward—Room 303. There's a woman in the fetal position sleeping on the edge of her bed.

She continues down the hall to the nursery. His forehead is against the glass keeping him apart from his new born daughter.

"Which one is yours," she asks the new dad.

He doesn't lift his head. "Second row, dead center." He beams. He's either been smiling or crying the last two days and both have yet to subside.

"She's beautiful. What's her name?"

His fondness is coupled with the aura of untapped possibilities as a new father. Then the floor starts to shake haphazardly.

"What the..." The man pushes through the stranger to get to his daughter and protect her from whatever is coming.

I'm coming. I'm coming.

"Cole. Cole, wake up. Wake up now!"

I stagger awake to Ava hovering over me and shaking me violently. That was the shaking in my dream. My wife probably needs a bowl of Hot Cheetos mixed in ramen. I read food cravings continue postpartum. I square my eyes on Ava and see she's scared. I boost myself up, alert.

"What's happened?"

"Something is wrong. Something bad," she says.

I leap out of Ava's bed and run through the hallways and staircases in my socks to get to the nursery. There's a group of nurses huddled inside behind the glass where sleeping babies lie. Our nurse turns to me with blood shot eyes.

She slowly makes her way out of the nursery to come and stand in front of me. I look over her head to the single empty bassinet. Hesitantly, she wraps her arms around my waist. I stand cold in her warm embrace, unwilling to believe the unthinkable.

The elevator dings behind us and Ava wheels herself out. I remove myself from the nurse and fall in front of Ava to stop her from coming any closer. I can't let her see the vacant crib where our newborn daughter is not sleeping with her hands tucked under her chin, the way I left her.

"I'm sorry—" I blubber. "I'm so sorry." I set my head in her lap and cry.

Forty two hours ago, I promised I would protect my daughter against the obstacles she'd encounter. Six months ago I promised Ava in front of the Indianapolis marital court with Nugget and Gail as our loathing witnesses that I'd love and protect her for the rest of our lives.

Thinking Casey was the worst of our fate, I was prepared to bake cookies, attend PTA meetings, save for college. Missing children are gone for years, without parents knowing how or why. I do not know how I am going to get Ava back—get myself back from an eternal darkness such as this.

"Cole, stop. Stop crying," Ava says, pushing my head from her lap.

An expression mixed with fury, rage, and fortitude etch her face to the point where I barely recognize her. I wipe my eyes for clarity as to why I'm the only one suffering.

"I don't know where my daughter is," she says. "But I do know who took her."

TO BE CONTINUED...

BOOK TWO

You Promise is book one in a duology.

Book Two to come.

Thank You

Thank you for reading:)

Please consider leaving a review so I may get the chance to reach more readers.

Acknowledgments

Dear reader,

I cannot thank you enough for reading my sophomore novel and coming all the way to the acknowledgments for more rambling.

You Promise is a story I've had on my heart for awhile. Before becoming an indie author, I tried the querying process (when I was coming up, self-publishing was highly frowned upon). With a horde of rejections and one manuscript request that didn't go anywhere, I—again, gave up writing. *You Promise* came back to me when I was thinking to myself 'ooo, I want to re-read that book with the evil twin, the good twin and that girl.'

After searching through my reading tracker, I remembered 'that book with the evil twin, the good twin and that girl' was something I wrote! This exact scenario happened with my debut, *Better Luck Next Time*, as well.

All that to say, I am so proud of myself for getting *You Promise* published so I may now re-read it whenever I want.

Did I write *You Promise*? Yes. However, the time I was able to put into this novel, my writing in general, and my new bookstore (BOOKS+), wouldn't be possible without the loml. He is certainly my anchor in this sea of life.

Mommy, Granny—y'all are the greatest women I'm honored to look up to.

Azaria POOKIE Brown, thank you for always leveling me up in writing and life.

Jensen Parker, thank you for having the answers to all of my questions, no matter the time of day. Sophie B. Murphy, thank you for seeing me the way I am, your friendship means the world.

To the community I have and the community to come, I love you all. I want all your dreams to come true.

SIGN UP

Sign up for my monthly newsletter. Subscribers are **first** to know release dates, upcoming events, etc.

taylorjbridgeforth.com

Also By
Taylor J. Bridgeforth

Better Luck Next Time 1
Coming Up Dana 1.5

You Didn't Tell (a novella)

You Promise Book 1

ABOUT THE AUTHOR

Taylor J. Bridgeforth multitasks as an author, reader, podcast host, YouTuber and bookstore owner (BOOKS+). Outside of those immediate interests, she likes to sing karaoke, play Mario Kart, travel, nap and eat. Taylor lives in Indianapolis, IN with her family.

www.taylorjbridgeforth.com